BLAZING

KYLIE GILMORE

Blazing: © 2021 by Kylie Gilmore

Cover design by: Michele Catalano Creative

Published by: Extra Fancy Books

ISBN-13: 978-1-64658-029-3

Blaze of glory! Or a blazing hot mess.

1

Max

The irony of driving down Lovers' Lane to plow snow for a woman I wanted the moment I set eyes on her isn't lost on me. First, because we could never be lovers—Brooke Winters is engaged. Second, because I've got those Bellamy genes, which means commitment is not my thing. It all goes back to Dad walking out when I was eight, saying he was drowning in responsibilities. People say I'm a lot like him—laid-back, always looking for a good time. What they really mean is irresponsible. It's probably why I'm still single.

I pull up to the old Dutch farmhouse, a two-story cedar-shingled home with a large addition on the side. This place predates the town, built in the 1700s. It's got good bones, but I imagine the inside needs a lot of work to turn it into a bed and breakfast. That's what sisters Brooke and Paige plan to do with it. I only met them once, a couple of months back. Their brother called me early this morning to get out here and plow after a freak March snowstorm buried Summerdale, New York, under eighteen inches of snow. It was a lot more snow than predicted.

I position my pickup truck, lower the plow attached to the front, and get started clearing the driveway. A glimpse of red catches my eye. There's a woman in a beige wool coat with a red scarf wrapped around her head digging snow away from the front door with a tiny shovel. Probably Brooke or Paige. I can't see her face. Is she using an ice scraper from her car?

I crane my neck and spot a black Mazda parked behind a snow hill created by the town's plow at the end of the cul-de-sac. That's not a good place to park. The wind will blow snow on the car, and if the town's truck comes by to drop sand on the road, the driver might not see it.

I put the truck in Park, power down the window, and lean out. The wind whips snow around my face. "Hey!"

The brunette woman continues industriously shoveling with her ridiculously tiny shovel. Little Red Riding Hood comes to mind, eager to get inside and meet the big bad wolf. Instead she's got me, big but not bad. I've been told I'm charming.

I turn off the truck and get out, walking over to her. "Hey there!"

She whirls, holding a...dog brush? I stifle a laugh. It's Brooke, the engaged woman I have to pretend no more than a friendly interest in. I met her two months ago when she showed up at our town's Winterfest. She was with her dog, Scout, a golden retriever with no discernible talent, whom she entered in the Dog's Got Talent contest. Scout was all over me. Too bad that didn't lead to an easy in with Brooke. Her sparkly diamond engagement ring practically shouted to keep my distance. Didn't stop me from looking.

"Hi," she says, her green eyes boring into mine with a steely look. "Don't you dare laugh. My ice scraper broke this morning when I cleared off my car. This is the only tool I have available." She pauses. "Did Wyatt send you?"

"Sure did." I offer my gloved hand. "I'm Max Bellamy." I don't assume she remembers me from two months ago, though her pretty face seems to be imprinted on my brain.

She shakes my hand. "Brooke. Wyatt's always one step ahead, big bro taking care of us. Anyway, I bought this place."

I nod. "We met once before at the Dog's Got Talent contest at Winterfest back in January."

She looks thoughtful and then beams a smile that takes

her from pretty to beautiful. My pulse thrums through my veins. "Oh yeah! The bearded wonder. You look different with the hat covering your hair. I remember Scout wouldn't leave you alone. That was embarrassing. I've never seen Scout react like that to someone."

I grin. "Bearded wonder?"

She looks up at me under her lashes. My heart kicks up a notch. "You must be a wonder, at least to him."

"Guess you left him home."

She gestures vaguely toward the street. "He's at Wyatt's house, where I'm staying when I'm in town."

"Well, you can put away your dog brush, the bearded wonder has a snowblower and shovel in the truck. I'll clear a path to the front door in no time."

"Thank you." She exhales sharply, her breath forming a puff in the cold air. "Today has been a disaster from start to finish. We're supposed to start renovations after months of waiting on permits, I took two weeks off work to make sure things went smoothly, and now the construction crew can't make it up here from New Jersey."

"Why didn't you hire local?"

She tosses a hand in the air, and the dog brush goes flying toward me. "Oh!"

I catch it right before it hits my chest.

"Sorry! First my dog won't stop climbing you, and now I throw a brush at you."

I hand it back, our eyes meeting up close, and a flicker of primal recognition flashes between us. Her lips part. Attraction. *Mutual* attraction.

I ease back a step. No way I'm messing around with a woman who's engaged. Don't need the drama, especially when most of my clients are in this small community, where word travels fast.

She blinks a few times. "In answer to your question, I didn't use a local crew because I knew Gage's company through my architecture firm in New Jersey. I trust him. The roads aren't clear for him to make it today, but he'll be here tomorrow."

I glance at the skinny path she dug about four inches down in the snow. "So you were shoveling out the front door for the crew's arrival tomorrow?"

She holds up a palm. "I know I look like a nut out here digging with a dog brush, but I was just so eager to get inside to see the place again. And I planned to get a few more pictures before they start demo. I already have pictures, of course, to figure out the renovation budget, but I was anxious to get more before it's gutted. I'm hoping to get the inn featured in an architecture magazine, which would bring good buzz." She sounds really worked up about the project. No doubt it's a huge undertaking.

"Cool."

She gestures toward the street. "So I guess I'll go wait in my car for you to finish up here."

"Pull it into the driveway after I leave. That's a bad spot where you parked. It could get hit by the town's sanding truck."

"Will do!"

She steps toward me. I step to her right to get out of the way just as she steps with me. We do a little dance, trying to move around each other, and somehow manage to keep getting in the other's way. It would be funny except I like having her near a little too much.

She halts and holds up a hand near my chest. Her face framed by the red scarf is striking—fair skin with pink cheeks from the cold, her green eyes standing out in contrast. "If you could just go back that way. I figure it's easier for me to take the path you already took, and the driveway is half clear, so…"

"Right." I mentally shake my head at my own distraction. I turn, heading back to my truck.

I wait for her to get out to the street before I go back to work. As I plow near the end of the long driveway, I get a good look at the back of the property. It's huge. Acres of what was once farmland backing onto woodland. The front yard is also large, the house set back from the street. Now this could be a major client for Bellamy Landscapes. I hope she hasn't already hired a landscape design company from New Jersey because I'm eager to put my hat in the ring.

I need the business to help my older brother, Liam, save his farm in Vermont. He called yesterday, urging me to sell the house that's been in our mother's family for generations. My brother, sister, and I inherited it from Mom when she passed two years ago, though I'm the only one who lives there. It's an original lakeside cottage from the 1960s when Summerdale was first founded by hippies as a type of utopian community. My grandfather helped build it. The house needs renovations, but it's on prime real estate on the shore of Lake Summerdale and would likely sell for a decent amount.

Thing is, I don't want to sell. Not only is the house our family legacy, but for me, it's an ideal location for my business, and I have my best family memories there. If I could buy out Liam's share with some much-needed business, it would fix everything. I can't take out a loan against the house because Liam wants to cash out, not be tied to more debt. He can't get another loan for his farm, so I'm going to try for a personal loan later today as a backup plan to my *drumming up new business fast* plan.

He's given me a month to either cough up the money for his share or sell the house. He's not playing hardball. That's how long he has before he's in serious financial trouble. And, no pressure, but he just found out his live-in girlfriend is pregnant. He has no plans to marry her, but he doesn't want to be homeless either. Irresponsible Bellamy genes shining through.

Once the driveway's clear, I get the snowblower out of the back of my pickup truck to clear the front walk. Hope fills me just looking around the size of this property. Maybe I won't end up drowning in debt or be forced to sell the house. I'll ask Brooke about landscaping as soon as I finish.

∾

Brooke

I sit in my car, warming up my frozen fingers, and glance back at Max making short work of clearing the front walk. It's almost like a snowblower works better than a dog brush in the snow. Ha! I shake my head, still a little embarrassed over that one. Before Max arrived, I even attempted to dig snow away from the door with my gloved hands, but my fingers got too cold. Not my finest moment. I've just been so anxious over my first project as lead architect, and the stakes have never been higher. Not only did Paige and I pour our life savings into the inn, big sis was able to contribute more money and cut her hours back at work to commit more time. We're equal partners despite that disparity, which only adds more pressure. I have to prove she made a good choice going into business with me.

Did I mention my big sis is tough as nails?

I love her, obviously, or I would never have ventured into business with her. I've been counting down the days to get started, and I couldn't let a freak snowstorm keep me from doing something, *anything* to move forward. The Inn on Lovers' Lane has to be a success. I'm going to do everything in my power to bring this renovation in on time and on budget.

A few minutes later, I spot Max approaching my car. I suck in air as he comes into view. He's more than a bearded wonder. He's *gorgeous*. Tall, wide shoulders, blue eyes that sparkle with good humor. He's wearing a blue plaid flannel jacket, black jeans, and black boots, and I'm willing to bet he's got many fine muscles hiding under there from his hard physical labor working on landscape stuff. His truck says Bellamy Landscapes on the side. Too bad I'm off men.

I'm jaded, I admit it. I always seem to attract the wrong man. Usually, just when I think things are going well with a guy, they cheat on me or they ghost me, not bothering to show up for a date and ignoring my calls and texts. And then, of course, there are the guys who act serious but only want sex, which I find out afterward as they sprint out the door, never to be seen again. Even instituting a four-date rule before sex didn't stem the tide of *screw and go* guys. Do I attract the worst, or is it just guys my age are terrified of commitment? Is it so much to ask to find a nice guy to settle down with? I'm twenty-seven, and I'm ready for something lasting.

Anyway, I couldn't figure out the solution to the guy problem, so I just stepped out of the dating-mating game. That's why I wear Paige's old engagement ring to ward off men.

I power down the window as Max gets close. "Hi, all finished?"

"Yup, you can go in. Mind if I take a look around with you?"

"Uh." I'm flustered and can't think of a single reason why he *shouldn't* join me other than I'd like to avoid a guy I find attractive. I can't afford a distraction at this critical time for the inn, and I'm definitely not willing to risk another disappointment. How do I say you're too attractive to be around without sounding like I'm coming on to him?

He continues, his voice smooth as silk. "I've lived here all my life and never seen the inside. I'm curious."

I take off my gloves, being sure to move my hand so the diamond engagement ring sparkles. It's my anti-man shield. Thank goodness Paige's fiancé left the country before their wedding. *Sorry, Paige!* "Sure, why not."

"Great." He opens my door for me and offers his hand to help me out.

I ignore his helpful hand and get out on my own. He shuts the door for me. *Nice manners.*

Nope, doesn't matter. You're off men for a reason.

Isn't three and a half months long enough? We have needs down here.

No can do. Remember Rick? Cheating and acting like I was crazy for calling him on it. I saw them together.

We have nee-ee-ds!

"So what kind of plans do you have for the place?" Max asks, interrupting my conversation with my nether regions.

"So many plans," I say, trying to bring my mind back to its usual orderly place. "When the renovation's complete, we'll have five guest rooms and an apartment for the innkeeper. That'll be my sister Paige. I'll be working here part-time."

"You must be close with your sister."

"Mmm, yeah. I mean, we had our share of fights as kids. A particularly nasty time when we were teens, but now that we're adults, we're close."

"Nasty like pulling each other's hair, or was it more the silent treatment?" He gives me a lopsided smile that warms me. "Which I hear can be just as deadly."

I laugh. "Pulling hair, yelling, and throwing things. We're only two years apart and both headstrong. My younger sister, Kayla, is the sweet one. Do you have a sister? You seem to know about normal sister behavior."

"I do. Younger than me. She had me and my older brother, so I never got to see the sister-fight action."

We head up the nicely cleared and salted front walk to my new inn. The cedar siding is in good shape, and the roof was replaced five years ago. I stand taller, filled with pride. The inn will be my first glorious success as lead architect.

I pull the key from my purse and open the front door. I step inside to the living room, pleased that it's still warm in here. We left the heat on low so the pipes wouldn't freeze and burst.

Max steps in behind me. "Hello, 1970s."

I laugh. "The wood paneling is actually from the 1950s. The previous owner was an elderly woman, who had to be moved to assisted living. She had dementia. The house has been in her family since it was built. Can you believe that? Hundreds of years of the same family living here."

Max runs his hand along the wood paneling. "Family legacy. A shame they had to sell."

"She never had kids, and there was no next of kin who wanted it."

I glance around, mentally cataloging what we'll be doing in the living room. The original hardwood floors are in good condition for the most part, just need a few replacement boards. We'll restore the older windows, which aren't original but antique. The original post and beam ceiling looks great, just a touch-up on the beams. After we take down the wood paneling on the walls, I'm hoping to find the plaster underneath is in good shape.

The major upgrades will be for the kitchen, bedrooms, and bathrooms. We'll need to add bathrooms as well. Then there's also upgrades for electrical, plumbing, and to add air-conditioning. Fortunately, the well and septic system were already large enough to handle the inn's needs. I bite back a smile and bounce on the balls of my feet. The house has a lot going for it already, and I'll take it the rest of the way.

"You look like you have a vision for the place," Max says.

"Sure do. Feel free to look around while I take pictures."

He lifts his palms. "Anything I should watch out for? Weak floorboard? Raccoons?"

I smile. "Everything's in working condition. We had the whole place scrubbed top to bottom after the previous owner's furnishings were cleared out. Pretty sure the raccoons moved on to a better neighborhood."

He cocks his head. "Better than Lovers' Lane? I don't know. I've heard there's quite a few raccoons honeymooning around here."

"Best garbage in town, huh?"

He flashes a smile that reaches his blue eyes, tiny crinkles forming at the corners. "Gourmet meal out."

Warmth floods me at that smile, my pulse thrumming. Nope. Not happening. I dig into my purse for my digital camera and start taking pictures.

Max wanders to my left. "Whoa. These stairs are narrow." He appears back in the living room. "Were people short and thin in ye olden days to fit on those stairs?"

"Not unless they were malnourished. They built the stairs narrow because the staircase is supported by the walls on either side. Space was at a premium in these old structures. Modern stairs take up a lot more space."

"Huh. You know your stuff."

"I hope so. Otherwise, the five years to get an architecture degree, three years of training, and passing a six-part exam would've been just so Mom had something to tell the neighbors."

He laughs. "You're funny."

I lift one shoulder. "Probably won't be once things get going here. A lot of pressure on me to get this right, on time and on budget. We poured our life's savings into it."

He whistles in low sympathy before heading back toward the stairs.

I move on to the kitchen and snap more pictures just to be sure I have a good amount of before pics for a possible feature article. There's a few prestigious architecture magazines that could be interested, as well as regional magazines for visitors to the area. Maybe the inn will even be the cover story! I so missed being here. I haven't been at our property in a month because I've been so busy at work, moving into Mom's house to save money on rent, and planning for this place.

The kitchen looks like it could be on a 1950s sitcom with an old glossy white refrigerator, dusty rose cabinets, and linoleum floor. I hate to let the old appliances go, but for this to be a proper bed and breakfast, we'll need to upgrade to a gourmet kitchen and expand it out the back. Our plan is to hire a chef as a consultant to set up the menus for breakfast and teach me and Paige how to make the dishes. We can't afford to put a chef on payroll permanently. One day.

A short while later, Max joins me again downstairs, where I'm imagining a seating arrangement around the original hearth in the den.

"Thanks for the tour," he says.

I turn. "Self-guided tour. No problem at all. Did you check out the addition? That's where the largest suite and innkeeper's apartment will go. There's a door through the dining area."

He shakes his head. "That's okay. The original house is enough. Have you come up with plans for the grounds? Maybe a vegetable garden for the kitchen, a koi pond with a waterfall for guests to relax around, perennial plantings."

I stare at him. "Sounds like you've given it some thought.

We planned on a private doggie play area for guests since we're going to be a dog-friendly B&B."

His brows lift. "Oh, yeah? Cool. I'm sure that will be popular. Have you hired a landscape design firm?"

"No, not yet. That's Paige's department. She's looking into a few."

He brightens. "I'm your guy." He pulls his wallet from his back jeans pocket and fishes out a business card, handing it to me. "You have a great property with a lot of potential. I can make it a dream for your guests. Also, I'm local and the owner, so you can call me any time day or night if there's an issue. Could I draw up a proposed plan and present it to you and Paige?"

I look over his card while I try to think of a reason to tell him no. He has a website, which Paige prefers, so she can see his past work. Ah, hell. I don't want to be prejudiced against him just because he's gorgeous. Beautiful people need clients too.

"And I have experience with large properties," he adds. "I'm working on the Bell estate right now. Still have room in the schedule for you though. I have a crew of four plus me. The Bell estate is in town, where the royal ball was held for Winterfest. I saw you there."

"You did?"

His lips curve up. "You're hard to miss."

I flush, my heart kicking up. I hadn't noticed him there. I was too busy biting my nails over whether our offer would be accepted on the inn. I only went to the ball because my younger sister, Kayla, insisted I go since I was in town. She lives here with her fiancé, Adam. I think she was hoping I'd meet a local guy and hit it off with them. Nope. She's a romantic since she fell madly in love. She doesn't understand why I'm still wearing my anti-man shield. It's a pretty shield —a gold band with a round sparkly diamond.

I look up into Max's eager expression and cave. "Sure, we'd love to hear your proposal."

"Great. Thanks so much. How's Thursday to meet? Any time after four works for me."

"Thursday would be perfect. Paige leaves for her job in the city on Friday." New York City being "the city" to us. Paige is a real estate broker working only weekends now, so she can spend more time here.

I hold up his card. "I'll call you after I talk to her for a definite time."

"Great." He offers his hand to shake. I place my hand in his, and a zing of sensation rushes up my arm at contact. Much different experience than with my gloves on. His hand is warm and strong as it envelops my smaller hand in a firm shake.

He drops his hand and takes a quick step back. "I'd better get to work on that." He turns and strides to the front door. Then he stops and turns back. "Thanks, Brooke. I appreciate the opportunity."

"Of course."

He flashes a smile, turns, and walks out the door.

My pulse kicks up at that smile. I didn't say I'd definitely hire him. He was just so happy for the chance. It makes me think he could really use the work. Actually, that can be a good thing. He'll make an effort to do the job right.

And, if we're working together professionally, that takes his gorgeousness right out of the equation. I'd never get involved with someone on my payroll. A koi pond with a waterfall sounds nice. And a vegetable garden could complement our breakfast offerings. Fresh herbs, scallions, onions, potatoes. My mind is already racing with ideas. Paige and I only talked about cleaning up the landscaping, planting some new stuff, and a dog play area.

Now I just have to convince Paige these cool additions to the property will be a good investment for us. I put a hand to the side of my neck. And convince my pulse to stop racing every time Max smiles.

2

Max

    I tap the steering wheel rapidly on the drive over to Wyatt's place, adrenaline racing through me. A lot rides on how my proposal goes over tonight. Three days ago, Brooke emailed me a survey map of the property, and I've been hard at work coming up with a comprehensive landscape design plan ever since. I need this one. My personal loan was turned down at the bank. I have too little savings and too much debt on my business from landscape equipment and trucks to qualify. No kidding. I pour all my money back into my business. My clients are mostly local residential customers, but now with the Bell estate and possibly the inn, Bellamy Landscapes could grow to the next level.

    My brother's situation is never far from my mind. Struggling farm and a pregnant girlfriend. He grows hay, and when he stopped using chemicals on it, eighty percent of the hay died. He's talked to other farmers and found a young couple who did similar and restored the hay fields by bringing in chickens, turkeys, and sheep. Something about the animals grazing and fertilizing that helps the hay fields. He needs the money to buy animals and to tide him over until the hay fields are replenished. Not only is the new animal method more ecofriendly than chemicals, but he can also sell meat, eggs, and wool. If I could help him without selling the house, he'll be fine in the long run.

I exhale sharply, sorely regretting giving the Bell estate a thirty percent discount on updating the landscaping on their property. I only did it as a favor to my friend Sloane. The Bell estate is rented out for events, and Sloane booked it for Winterfest's royal ball. I negotiated a reduced price on their catering in exchange for the landscaping discount. Sloane and her dad are like family to me. Not that I ever told them that.

Sloane's dad, Rob Murray, is real salt of the earth. He's been a second dad to me over the years. He gave me my first job in high school, working at his auto repair shop, and taught me everything I know about cars. Truth is, I knew next to nothing when I started. I convinced him to hire me, saying I was a quick learner and willing to work hard. Looking back, he probably saw a scrappy teenaged boy in need of money. Things were tight on Mom's secretary salary. Dad never sent child support. In fact, we never saw him again. Irresponsible, like I said.

Not only did Rob give me a job when I needed it most, he still welcomes me back for shifts at his shop in the winter when my landscaping business is slow. If I could choose a dad, I'd choose him.

I turn onto the long uphill driveway leading to Wyatt's place. Word around town is that he's a retired billionaire from some kind of tech start-up. He's in his early thirties. Must be nice. I pass a gray lighthouse on my right on the landlocked property. It's actually a water tower decorated like a lighthouse, as Wyatt shares with anyone who asks. He loved the irony and says it's the main reason he bought the house.

I park the truck and grab a binder of photos and the cardboard tube holding my landscape drawings. I'm self-taught, but I think I have a good eye for it. At least my local clients always seem satisfied. This is next level though. I've never done a huge project like this one. The Bell estate already had landscaping in place. I just freshened it up. Though I did convince them to replace a crumbling concrete pathway with stone tiles.

I take a deep breath and get out of the truck. Good fortune favors the bold, right? Or is that the brave? Bah. Doesn't matter. I'm both.

Wyatt's house is a large two-story with gray clapboard siding. I've been here before. Sloane again. She invited me here for a photo shoot for her boyfriend's charity calendar to raise money for our local animal shelter. It was one shirtless guy with a dog per month. Not exactly my scene, but I have a soft spot for Sloane obviously. She's like a little sister to me. Same deal with my own little sister, Skylar, who adores me. Not just my ego talking here. She tells me that without a trace of irony. Skylar just says whatever with no filter, but in a good way. She's like a ray of sunshine.

Thinking of Skylar's unconditional adoration calms me, almost like she's cheering me on. *Of course you can do this, Max! You're the best.* If I get this job, I'll try to bring her on board at the inn. Maybe Brooke and Paige could use an interior designer too.

I reach the blue front door and ring the bell.

The dogs raise a furious chorus of barks. It's just a little white shih tzu and a sweet pit bull mix. This is their *someone's at the door* behavior. They did it for every new guy who showed up for our photo shoot for the charity calendar.

The door opens to Wyatt, a guy about my height with rumpled brown hair, brown eyes, and a trimmed beard. He's got the shih tzu under one arm and the pit bull by the collar. Scout, Brooke's golden retriever, lunges for me, standing up on my leg. I shake him off.

"Stand down," Wyatt tells the dogs, who immediately quiet. He turns to me. "Hey, Max, come on in. Paige and Brooke are waiting for you at the kitchen table."

I step inside. "Thanks."

He sets the shih tzu down and gestures for me to follow. The dogs circle around to sniff me. Scout keeps bumping my hand with his muzzle for pets. I can only give him a short stroke over the head with my drawings tucked under my arm.

"Done any more shirtless photo shoots lately?" Wyatt asks.

"Ha. No." I follow him down the front hallway, trying not to step on the shih tzu. The other dogs are behind me now, trying to sniff my ass. I hurry forward. "That was a one-off."

"Yeah, me too, but it was for a good cause."

"Scout, come!" a woman calls. Probably Brooke.

Scout bolts past us, and the other dogs race after him. Guess Scout's the alpha of this pack.

"I heard they plan to break ground on the new animal shelter in May," I say, since we're talking about the charity calendar for it.

He grins over his shoulder. "I heard that too."

Sloane says she suspects Wyatt anonymously donated the amount needed after our fundraising efforts to make the shelter happen. He hasn't admitted it to anyone, but he's the only one in town who could've come up with that kind of cash. His grin just now tells me it was definitely him.

I step into a modern kitchen done in white and gray. My gaze zeroes in on Brooke sitting at a large light wood table in a dining area across from the kitchen. I glimpse her sister in the periphery of my vision, but I can't tear myself away from Brooke. I've thought about her more than I should.

She stands, and my mouth goes dry. Her pink and white ribbed sweater clings to her curves, and her dark jeans are tight on that sexy body. I tell myself to focus on her engagement ring, but my gaze travels back up her body to her green eyes. Stunningly beautiful from head to toe.

I suck in air, suddenly off-balance. Scout knocked into the back of my knee. He's circling me, wagging his tail. Then he jumps on my leg, arching his head up for pets.

"Scout!" Brooke exclaims. "So sorry, Max." She rushes over and grabs him by the collar, ordering him to sit. He does. She meets my eyes. "You must smell good to him. He doesn't usually act like this."

"The bearded wonder smells like fresh meat," I quip.

She laughs. "Right. Something like that. Anyway, thanks for coming."

Wyatt calls the dogs, shaking a closed hand, probably holding treats because the dogs make a beeline for him and follow him out of the kitchen.

"Can I get you anything to drink?" she asks with a sweet smile.

I jolt back to reality. Time to win my biggest client ever that I desperately need so I don't end up losing the family home or let down my brother with his struggling farm and pregnant girlfriend. No pressure. "I'm good, thanks. I'm ready to jump in and show you my proposal."

Brooke gives me a bland professional smile this time, like she just remembered my purpose here too. "Sure."

She walks over to the kitchen table, and I follow. "Paige, this is Max Bellamy of Bellamy Landscapes. Max, my sister Paige."

I turn my attention to her sister. Paige's brown hair has highlights in it and is shorter than her sister's with some curl to it. She's fully made up, wearing a sleeveless white V-neck shirt with a cherry pattern. Brooke has a much more natural look. I immediately peg Paige as high maintenance, the kind of woman who goes to the salon on the regular and fusses with her makeup and creams endlessly. What can I say? I know women.

I walk over and offer my hand to Paige. "Great to meet you."

Her brown eyes are sharp and assessing, scanning my expression and taking a quick glance at my shirt. "You too."

I'm suddenly glad I took the time to trim my beard and put on a collared shirt with trousers and leather shoes. Hope I passed inspection.

Brooke gestures for me to sit in the chair across from Paige and takes a seat at the head of the table, adjacent to me. I set my binder on the table, which is a collection of labeled pictures of plantings, and take the rolled-up drawings from the cardboard tube out and spread them across the table.

Paige immediately turns the plans to face her, and Brooke shifts them so they're at an angle she can see too.

"A little about me," I say. "I'm the owner of Bellamy Landscapes. We've been in business for eleven years with a regular roster of local clients, as well as work on larger projects like yours. I have a crew of four plus myself, and we do everything from landscape design to gardens to mowing and plowing."

"Wyatt hired him to plow the inn out for us during that snowstorm," Brooke says.

I smile, remembering her shoveling with her little dog brush. I'm tempted to tease her about it. Not the time.

"I mostly saw private homes on your website," Paige says.

"Yes, that's been most of my clientele, but like I told Brooke—" I glance at her, and she smiles encouragingly "—we're working on the Bell estate right now—"

"Why isn't it on your website?" Paige asks.

"It's not finished yet. I like to put the before and after pictures up."

"Stop interrupting him," Brooke says. "I want to hear about the plan."

Paige shoots her an annoyed look, and Brooke sends her a fierce look in return. *Sisters.*

I continue. "This top page is a view of the front area of the inn." I get up and walk over to stand between the sisters to point out things on the drawing as I talk. I warm to my topic, genuinely enthusiastic about the look and feel the landscaping can convey when visitors first approach. Native plantings that blend with the natural environment but also say welcoming B&B in the country. There's plenty of people in the city who'd enjoy all the fresh air and nature we have here.

Paige interrupts constantly with questions, which I seem to answer to her satisfaction. Brooke just listens.

By the time I get to the back property, Brooke is smiling and nodding. Paige remains stone-faced.

I finish and take my seat. I open my binder. "This shows what the plantings would look like at different times of the year. Some nice colors for spring, summer, and fall."

"Ooh, I like the idea of changing looks with the season," Brooke says.

Inspiration hits. "My team could even decorate the outside for Christmas if you'd like—wreathes, greenery, lights, you name it." We've never decorated for Christmas before, but now that I think about it, why not? Business is slow in the winter except for plowing. That could be another source of revenue for us with busy families, even local business owners. I'm a genius.

"I can decorate," Paige says. "I regularly stage apartments and condos for my other job. Decorating is not what we need."

"Right," I say. "No problem. Let's take a look at the New York fern. By the way, these are deer-resistant plants. They don't like the taste of them."

"How about for dogs?" Paige asks.

"I don't think dogs eat plants," Brooke says. "Scout couldn't care less if I drop a piece of lettuce."

"I'll look into that before we go forward," I say.

By the time I've finished, I'm pumped full of energy for this cool project. I can't read Paige at all. Brooke looks pleased, though it's clear she won't make a move without her sister. Time to close the deal.

"I can start as soon as next week. I'd begin with any needed excavation, clean up what's there already, and then work on any hardscaping needed, like the dog play area, the curved path to the back yard, the patio, and koi pond. I'd want to wait a couple of weeks for new plantings to ensure it's warm enough to sustain them overnight."

I pull the cost estimate from the back of the binder. I wasn't exactly sure how to price a project like this. I did cost and labor plus my usual fifteen percent markup. That's what I charge residential customers. I wasn't sure if a commercial project would go for more, and I didn't want to chance losing them when I need the business so urgently.

Paige looks over my cost estimates without a word and then passes it over to Brooke.

"Would you like to sign with me today, or do you need more time?" I ask, trying to hide my eagerness.

Paige flashes a smile and stands, offering her hand. "We'll call you."

Damn. That sounds like a no. I shake her hand. "Sure, thanks for your time. You can keep the plans to review."

I turn to Brooke to shake her hand. She ignores it, standing. "I'll walk you out."

I grab my stuff and walk out with Brooke. I want to ask her what she thought of my ideas, but I don't want to sound as desperate for the job as I am.

"It's a good plan," she offers. "I especially liked the privacy of the koi pond with the waterfall and stone benches."

"Thanks. It's good to have a few seating areas for your guests. Any idea on your time frame?" I get a ten percent deposit up front when they sign the contract, which may keep my brother from breathing down my neck. He said he'd give me a month, yet he keeps texting me other real estate listings in our area and what they sold for. He thinks I'm sitting on a gold mine. Obviously, he doesn't have any sentimental attachment to the house that's been in our family for generations. I guess he has bigger worries now.

"Landscaping isn't a priority, to be honest," Brooke says. "We're more concerned with renovating the inside."

"It would be good to have both parts moving along at the same time. I could start in the back of the property so I'm not in the way of the construction crew. It's a big job."

"I'll see what Paige says. She's in charge of the exterior. And we're still waiting on a permit for the dog play area. We just found out they need to have a public hearing with the neighbors on Lovers' Lane to see if it's okay."

"Plenty of other work to get started on." I stop by the front door and make one last bid for her business. "I'd love to be part of Summerdale's first inn."

She smiles, her green eyes dancing with good humor. "What about The Horseman Inn? I've heard it's been here for centuries."

"That was great for the colonial folk. It hasn't been an inn for more than a hundred years."

She cocks her head. "What's a horseman anyway?"

"According to my grandfather, the inn was named that to attract the drivers of horses as they made their way across the state. Stagecoaches often stopped in Summerdale on their way to New York City or the road farther north up to Boston."

"That makes total sense. How cool."

I double down on the history angle, since it seems like she likes it. "I'm a third-generation Summerdale resident. My grandfather was one of the original founders back in the sixties when they designed the town as a type of utopia. I live in the lakeside cottage he helped build."

Her face lights with interest. "Really? Oh, I'd love to see it. I've passed through Lakeshore Drive and saw some of the newer two-story homes, but there's only a few of the original one-story homes left. I bet it has some history."

It occurs to me I should've mentioned this during my presentation. Third-generation Summerdale resident shows that I know this town and want to help add to the town's appeal with the inn. "My house is in need of renovations, but you can't beat the view. Anytime you want to stop by, just let me know. You have my number on my card."

She presses her lips together. "I'd love to check out an original Summerdale structure, but it might have to wait. I do need to focus on the inn. I've got two weeks off work, and then I'm only going to be here part-time. I'm still full-time at my architectural firm in New Jersey with two days of remote work here Thursday and Friday."

"Sounds like two full-time jobs."

She lets out a breath. "Yeah, probably will be for a bit. Need the paycheck, though."

"Will you be full-time in Summerdale once the renovation's done?" It shouldn't matter since she's engaged, but I find myself hoping she'll be sticking around.

She nods. "I'd like to work part-time at the inn and take on local architecture clients on a part-time basis too. I'm especially interested in working on homes. *So* much more satisfying than my usual commercial office building work. It's what drew me to architecture in the first place."

I find myself leaning in. She smells like flowers. "That's great," I say with too much enthusiasm. Heat rises in my neck. "I mean, good for you."

She searches my expression before turning abruptly away and reaching for the door. Her diamond engagement ring catches the light. "Bye, Max. Thanks for stopping by."

I instantly deflate. No time frame. No signed contract. Big problem.

I force an upbeat tone. "Happy for the opportunity. Bye."

I step outside, my limbs heavy, and trudge back to my truck. Might be time to call a real estate guy.

3

Brooke

It's Friday afternoon, four days into my first solo architecture job, and I'm super pleased with the progress we're making. I knew hiring Gage was the right call. We're the same age, so I feel like we speak the same language. He's a natural leader, quick and decisive and, most importantly, competent. He's been running his own construction business since he was eighteen. I feel good knowing the renovation's in his capable hands when I have to scale back to part-time in a little more than a week.

Paige went back to the city for her real estate job. She wasn't ready to hire Max since she still had another landscaper lined up whom she wanted to talk to. I really liked Max's plan, and I especially liked that he's local and was so enthusiastic. All right, I just like him. He seems like a genuine, straightforward guy. I don't meet a lot of those. I can't imagine him ever ghosting someone.

I stare out at the backyard of the inn through the plastic tarp that used to be the back kitchen wall. I imagine Max there, working shirtless, muscles gleaming with sweat. *Yikes. Hello! Professional boundaries here.* I blame it on my long break from men and the fact that I'm new at being the boss. I never had to consider the complication of getting involved with someone I'm paying before. Anyway, Paige and I decided ahead of time that all major decisions have to be mutually agreed on, so hiring a landscaper is on hold until next week.

I walk around the kitchen space. The demo is finished, and it's just a shell with the back wall gone to make way for the expansion. Gage makes sure his crew cleans up every night before they go, so it's not too bad in here as far as dust and debris. I'm just making sure the bones are good before we put in the plumbing marks.

I turn and step into what will eventually be the dining room just off the large living room. Gage walks in with a grim expression on his face, holding a crowbar. Adrenaline fires through me at that expression. I immediately think of the budget and how much whatever problem he's found could throw us off schedule.

Actually, if I didn't know him from before, I'd find him a bit intimidating. He's a big guy, his short brown hair shaved on the sides, scruff on his jaw, bulging muscles in his red flannel shirt. His forearms, exposed from the rolled-up sleeves of his shirt, feature tattoos. I imagine more of him has ink as well, but I've never seen him without a shirt. He's attractive in a rugged way, if you don't mind the strong silent type. I prefer a guy who talks without prompting.

"What's up?" I ask.

"Mold in the basement from a pipe that burst down there previously. I'm not sure how far the mold spread. I'd like to pull down some of the wood paneling in the living room to check the wall interiors. The leak was right under the living room."

"The kitchen looked fine after demo," I say, desperately clinging to hope.

He inclines his head. "Let me assess the damage. Remediation is a must. You'll have to find someone local for that."

I cross my arms, hugging myself. "Sure, let's see what we've got."

He peels off a piece of wood paneling with the crowbar, and it splinters in half. "Cheap paneling," he mutters. He pulls a flashlight from his toolbelt and peers behind the space.

Then he pulls several more panels off until half the living room is torn down to the original crumbling plaster. He runs his palm along the plaster wall. There's no noticeable water stains.

"You mind if I cut a small hole in the plaster to take a look behind it?" he asks.

"Fine. We'll need to layer on fresh plaster anyway. These walls are original to the house."

He nods once. "You should clear out because of the dust. I'm going to get my saw and mask."

I swallow hard and walk out the front door. I'm already wearing a light jacket since it's cool in the house. I pace the side yard restlessly until I hear the saw roar to life, the sound jangling my nerves.

I move away, walking to the street and pacing in front of the house. Of course I expected there would be issues. No renovation project is easy, and I know it's an old farmhouse, but I really don't want to lose some of the features I planned. That's exactly what will happen if this puts us over budget. I'll have to cut elsewhere.

A short while later, Gage appears on the front porch, taking off his goggles and mask.

I hurry over to him. "Well?"

He cracks a rare smile. "No mold. The original lath and plaster behind the layers of plaster look sound too."

"Oh, thank God."

"Still need to do the mold remediation in the basement. We're lucky that it was probably a more recent issue; otherwise it could've spread."

"Any idea on cost or timeline?"

"Typically takes a few days for remediation and run you three thousand, give or take. We'll have to clear out while they do the work, so it'll set us back on the schedule. Call someone right away, and when you get a definite time, we'll work around it."

I try not to hyperventilate. The schedule is marked up perfectly to bring in various subcontractors at certain times. If I have to move the plumber, for instance, then that pushes everyone else back. I might not be able to get on their schedule again any time soon. Spring is a busy time for contractors.

"You okay?" he asks. "You look paler than usual." Gage doesn't mince words.

I paste on a smile. "Fine, thanks. I'll find someone for remediation and get back to you as soon as I know."

"Yup." He turns and goes back in the house.

I walk to my car, get inside, and grab my laptop case. This is my mobile office. *Not freaking out. Freaking out is the opposite of what's needed now.* I'll hold off on telling Paige the bad news until I know exactly how bad the news is.

I unzip my laptop case in jerky motions and turn the computer on. It takes forever to load. If I lose my shit now, then how am I going to manage the next three months? We're supposed to open in June in the hopes that a busy summer season will help pay our costs. I must remain cool, calm, and collected.

"Aahhh!" I let out a primal scream of frustration.

Forget the laptop. I pull out my phone for a quick Google search on mold-remediation costs in the area. Of course it's high. Everything in this part of the country is expensive. Sweat breaks out on my forehead. I never cared so much about a project until my own funds were on the line.

My email inbox is overflowing, but I ignore it. A few text notifications have me checking just in case it's important. My boss wants me to call in about CAD drawings I did before I left for my two-week vacation, Paige wants to know how it's going, Kayla's inviting me to lunch tomorrow, and there's an unknown sender.

I shoot back some quick replies and click on the unknown sender. *Hi, it's Max Bellamy. Hope you don't mind I asked Kayla for your number. Just wanted to follow up and see if you had any questions about my proposal.*

It's only been a day since he met with us. Wow. He must *really* need the work. I'm not even sure if we'll be able to do the full plan with him now. For sure, I'd rather let landscaping wait than have to scale back on the plans for the renovation.

I text him back: *Hi, Max. We may need to scale back on landscaping plans due to renovation issues. Paige has two more landscapers she's supposed to meet with on Monday. Will let you know.*

Max: *Hope it's nothing too major with the renovation. I'm sure an old house comes with a lot of challenges.*

I relax a little. I like the way he called it "challenges" instead of "major screwed-up disaster," which I have to admit was my first thought. For a moment, I consider venting to him. I don't want to unload on Paige because I'm eager to show her I can handle the job. I still want to prove myself to big sis. Sad but true. Knowing she put in more money and will soon be working at the inn full-time, I have to pull my weight.

I let out a breath. I don't know Max well enough for venting. I send him a quick thanks and step outside with my laptop, needing to cool off from my previous freak-out. I set the laptop on the trunk of my car and get to work. This *challenge* had better not screw everything up. How many more challenges will I have to deal with? Better if I don't know.

∾

Max

I take a seat on the deck of my house, taking in the view of Lake Summerdale. Early buds on the surrounding trees will soon burst into greenery. New life. Maybe it's time for me to make a change too. Why am I hanging onto this old wood-sided cottage by the lake? Nostalgia. Warm childhood memories.

Grandpop taking me out in a rowboat and teaching me to fish.

Dad teaching me how to swim. His cheers when I managed to doggy paddle on my first try.

Liam, me, and Skylar running around the beach. Swimming and splashing. Skylar inviting us to her fancy picnics with the fairies and leprechauns.

Fireworks on the Fourth of July with the whole family.

Mom decorating our floating creation for the end-of-summer regatta.

I shake my head. I'm an adult now. Grandpop and Mom passed away. I loved them both, and it's hard to let go of their legacy here at the cottage. Dad's a distant memory since I was eight the last time I saw him. I have to live in the now. I still don't have a big client to help dig me out of this situation, and now Brooke is saying they may have to scale back on landscaping due to renovation costs.

Since it's looking less likely I can get the money Liam needs, I need to at least look into the option of selling the house. No more hanging on for warm and fuzzy reasons. Fact is, I'm only part owner with my siblings, and one of the owners needs a fast sale, which is why I called a real estate guy on my lunch break earlier today. Still waiting to hear back from him. I gave my younger sister, Skylar, a heads-up on that. Her response? *We just gotta trust the universe, but I hope we can keep the house.* She has great memories here too.

A duck flies in for a landing and splashes in the lake, swimming around and dipping its head under water for dinner. Maybe Liam's wrong about the value of the house. Let's be honest. It was constructed in the sixties, and the only update was to the kitchen in the eighties. Dad worked construction, yet never renovated our house, preferring to collapse into his old recliner chair with a beer at the end of the day. The best part of the house is the deck, and even that can only fit four people comfortably. Inside, there's no central air-conditioning, just window air conditioners in the living room and my bedroom in the second-story attic space. Three bedrooms, living room, bathroom, kitchen, dining alcove, and a walk-out basement. Nothing spectacular besides the location.

My phone rings, and my gut tightens in anticipation of talking about selling my house. It's a local number. "Max Bellamy," I say.

"Hi, Max, this is Pete Faulkner returning your call. You'd like to sell your house?"

I let out a breath. "I'm just testing the waters at this point. I wanted to see what it might sell for before I decide."

"Where're you located?"

"Lakeshore Drive in Summerdale. It's one of the original cottages on the lake."

"Oh, wow, this is a rare find. There's only a handful of the original places left, and so few people ever sell on Lakeshore Drive. I can tell you right now, not even seeing it, that it'll fetch a good price. People from the city love to snatch these smaller homes up for a summer retreat."

My gut rolls. "Okay, so what's next?"

"I'll stop by tomorrow morning. I'll need pictures of the exterior and interior in daylight. I'm excited about this, and you called at the perfect time to sell. Spring is our biggest season for house shoppers."

Bile rises in my throat as I work out the time with him and give him the address. I hang up and close my eyes. I can't help but think Liam and Skylar will ultimately regret letting our lakeside cottage go. I know I will. We could never afford to buy here now, and it's part of our family history. A vision of Mom relaxing out here in her chaise lounge with a book and her big floppy hat flashes through my mind. She would often call out gentle reminders to me and Liam onshore to watch out for our little sister.

I rub my eyes. *Sorry, Mom.*

My phone rings again. Local number, but not the same as Pete's number. I answer, curious.

"Hi, Max. It's Audrey. I, uh, got your number from Kayla." That Kayla is quite the connector in town. She gave me Brooke's number too. Audrey Fox was my first love my senior year in high school. I ended it when she got into Columbia University because I hadn't wanted to hold her back. She's brilliant, and I believed she'd go far. Instead she returned to Summerdale after a semester to commute to the state university. Her dad lost his job, and they couldn't afford the tuition. By that time, I was with someone else. Despite living in the same town, Audrey and I have barely spoken more than a brief hello in years.

I sit up straighter. "It's good to hear from you, Aud."

"I wondered if you'd meet me for lunch tomorrow. I'd like to talk."

"About what?"

"Just some old stuff I'd like to better understand. I've had some time to think about it, and I think I was too harsh with you before. You know, when I yelled at you at ladies' night and called you Mr. Wrong."

She was harsh. A few months back, I ran into her at the bar at The Horseman Inn. She was drunk, but still sharp enough to yell at me, calling me Mr. Wrong and saying she didn't have time to waste on guys like me. She said her biological clock was ticking, and she wanted a husband and kids in that order. Then she yelled at me to go away. It stung. We used to be close.

Wait. She's not thinking of me as a candidate for husband and dad, is she? Doesn't she remember the Bellamy genes? Even after my serious relationship with Penny—five years—I couldn't bring myself to marry her. She wanted that; I couldn't do it. My brother's not the marrying type either, and Skylar is such a free spirit I can't imagine her ever settling down.

"Max?"

"Sure, that'd be great."

"Horseman at twelve."

"That works. I might be selling my house." My gut clenches just saying the words.

"Oh no! You love that house. *I* love that house. So cute, and the view is awesome."

I spill the whole story, telling her about what led me to this point. She's a good listener, warm and supportive. She tells me a bit about what she's been up to since we last really talked.

An hour later, I hang up, feeling a little lighter. The sun's setting over the lake. Two swans swim in the distance and then still, facing each other, their curved necks forming what looks like a heart. My pulse thrums a little faster. Maybe there's something between me and Audrey all these years later. It's been eleven years since our six-month relationship. We're both twenty-nine. Maybe we're in a place in our lives where the timing's finally right.

Biological clock.

I stand abruptly and go back inside the house. I told myself I'd never do the whole family thing. That's what made Dad leave—the overwhelming responsibilities of a wife, kids, bills. And everyone says I'm just like him.

I get a frozen burrito from the freezer and stick it in the microwave. My gourmet dinner. It couldn't hurt to have lunch with Audrey. I've missed her over the years despite seeing her around town. Audrey's the kind of person who only lets in a select few. I've been shut out for a long time. That's what I missed. Not our relationship so much as being part of her inner circle, where the smiles are frequent and she says more than *hello, how are you*.

I can admit it. Her sweetness is something I sorely need at the moment.

4

I head over to The Horseman Inn the next day, my mind buzzing. Pete stopped by this morning to take pictures of my house and give me his professional opinion on the value. And it was a whole helluva lot more than I would've guessed. The mortgage was paid off long ago, so the proceeds would be split three ways with my brother and sister. Enough for Liam to get those animals he needs to replenish the hay fields and to see him over the next year. I could pay off my business debt. Skylar could do whatever Skylar does, probably give it all to a good cause. In any case, it's the answer to a lot.

If only it didn't pain me to lose my family's legacy. Three generations living in that lakeside cottage.

I look around the restaurant for Audrey. It's Saturday, but it's not too crowded for lunch. She waves to me from a table by the window in the front dining room. Audrey hasn't changed much over the years. She's a petite five feet one with long black hair, blue eyes, and fair skin. She dresses modestly, usually in a blouse with trousers or skirt, though today she's wearing a soft-looking pink sweater. Her modest outfits don't mean she's a prude. She swears freely, and we had a lot of naked fun time too. I was her first.

I take a seat at the square dark wood table for two. "Good to see you."

She smiles sweetly. "You too. How'd it go this morning with Pete?"

I lean forward and whisper how much it's worth.

She claps a hand over her mouth, her blue eyes wide.

"I know. Purely based on the lakefront location. And also it's the right size for people in the city who want a second home for a summer retreat."

"Wow. So are you definitely selling?"

"I don't know. He said we should just list it, see what kind of offers I get, and then I can decide. Spring's the time for selling. I'm going to hold off as long as I can."

"Where would you go?"

I shrug. "Haven't figured that out yet. Not far. My business is here. Worst case, I'd crash with Rob Murray until I found a place of my own."

"He's been good to you," she says with a hint of the nostalgic memory I've been feeling the past couple of days. She knows I think of Rob as my honorary dad.

"Absolutely. Still helps me out, letting me work shifts in the winter at his shop when business is slow for me."

She studies me for a moment before grabbing a menu. "Let's eat, and then we'll talk."

"Sure."

Once we decide what we want, I look around for a waiter and spot Ellen, a woman in her sixties with a short head of dyed blond hair. She's been working here forever. She jerks her chin and walks over.

"Now isn't this a sight for sore eyes," Ellen says. "Max and Audrey back together. I remember when you used to come in here and share an order of fries, just talking each other's ears off."

I catch Audrey's eye. Hers look soft with memory. "Good times," I say. "We're just catching up today."

Ellen winks. "Sure, sure. What can I get ya?"

We order lunch—burger and fries for me, salad with chicken for her.

After Ellen leaves, Audrey gazes into my eyes. "We did have a good thing back then," she says softly.

I sit up straighter. *Is she hoping to get back together?*

"What about your biological clock?" I blurt.

"Shh! Oh my God, I can't believe you just said that." She glances around, but there's only one other couple in here. I don't recognize them.

"You said that when you yelled at me at ladies' night."

She leans across the table, gesturing me closer.

I lean in and whisper, "Is that what you wanted to talk about, your ticking biological clock? Can't help you there."

She rolls her eyes and whispers back, "I was going to wait until after lunch, but since you brought it up, I regret what I said to you that night. *All of it.* I had too much margarita—"

I grin. "You always were a lightweight. One wine cooler, and you were plastered."

"Yes, well, be that as it may. I was in a mood that night, sick of all the losers I was meeting through online dating. I took that out on you, and I apologize."

"No problem. I didn't give it another thought." *Maybe just a little.*

She leans back. "Really? I felt so bad."

I play it up. "It was the stuff of nightmares! I woke up in a cold sweat every night for weeks. Audrey yelled at me." I gesture like words are coming out of a cartoon mouth. "Mr. Wrong-Wrong-Wrong." I add the echo effect for emphasis.

She shakes her head, smiling. "As long as you weren't traumatized."

"Totally traumatized. Never gonna recover."

She looks down, tracing a finger across the top of the table. "I admit I was angry with you for a very long time. You broke up with me just as I got into my dream college. I didn't understand why because you could've visited me in the city. It was both the best and worst time of my life at once."

I get serious. "I know how smart you are, and I wasn't going anywhere, living at home, trying to get a landscaping business off the ground. I was mostly just mowing lawns for the first year. I didn't want to hold you back."

She meets my eyes, searching my expression. "Ironic that I ended up right back here working as a librarian. You must've thought I was going to set the world on fire when all I wanted was a quiet life surrounded by books."

I reach across the table and hold her hand, the gesture at once familiar and comforting. "Guess we should've communicated a little better. We both had a lot of growing up to do."

"Hi, Max! Hi, Audrey!"

I release Audrey's hand and turn to see Kayla with her sister Brooke. My gaze collides with Brooke's, and I'm suddenly alert and aware. Not because she's a potential client either. There's just something about her that draws me in. Her hair is up today, exposing her throat. A dark pulse throbs through me. She's in a white down jacket with jeans and black boots. Striking from head to toe. And by striking I mean damn sexy.

I keep a friendly tone. "Hey, good to see you two."

Audrey says something, but I can't focus on the words as Brooke approaches. She glances between me and Audrey and then turns her attention to Kayla.

"We're just having a girls' lunch, catching up," Kayla says brightly. "See you!"

"Us too," I say.

All of the women stare at me.

"Not a girls' lunch," I amend quickly. "We're catching up."

Kayla gives me a knowing look and winks. "Right. Totally get it. Enjoy your lunch!"

They move on to the back dining room.

Our food arrives a moment later, providing a much-needed distraction. I tell myself that Brooke's engaged and, even if she wasn't, I'm trying to get her business. What am I going to do, sleep with my most important client? Talk about messy. Not to mention her overprotective brother, Wyatt. If he likes you, as he currently likes me, he's pleasant and actually helpful, referring clients to me regularly. On the other hand, he's made it clear to everyone who knows him that you don't cross one of his beloved younger sisters without a major fight with him. Being a retired tech billionaire, Wyatt has the money and digital savvy to obliterate someone. Not a risk I'd like to take, thank you very much.

I take a big bite of burger, trying not to glance at the back dining room. I'm extremely conscious that Brooke is sitting there.

"How's your lunch?" Audrey asks.

"Good," I say around a mouthful of burger. "You like your salad?"

"Yeah, actually. Spencer, that's the new chef, he keeps it interesting. I've got pickled red onions, alfalfa sprouts, tiny grape tomatoes. Some kind of buttermilk ranch dressing. All in all, very tasty."

I nod and continue eating, my gaze trailing to the back room despite my best efforts not to look. Kayla's back is to us, partially blocking the view of Brooke. I glance over a few times, occasionally glimpsing Brooke smiling or laughing. It's nice to see her with her younger sister. They look close.

Just as we finish eating, Audrey says, "I remember you went to prom with Matt's younger sister. I always suspected you liked Livvie."

Oh-kay, so we're *really* rehashing old times. Guess Audrey needs to get it all out.

I take a drink of water and lean across the table. "Our breakup wasn't easy for me either, okay? I went with her because I didn't want to miss out on prom. All of my friends had dates, and she was a last-minute option. I knew she'd go since she was only a sophomore, and senior prom was a big deal. We didn't see each other after that. She never could've replaced you."

Her lips part, her eyes widening. "Oh, that's much nicer than what I thought you might say. I guess it stuck with me because I went with Dave, who'd just broken up with Sara, and then they got back together at prom. So there I was, alone, watching you with Livvie. She looked like she was having the time of her life."

I shrug. "She probably was. That doesn't mean I was."

She leans across the table, grabs me by the shirt, and kisses my cheek. "I feel better now, thanks."

I smile. "Glad I could clear that up after all these years."

Ellen sets the check down and moves on to the next table. I take out my credit card.

"I got it," Audrey says. "I'm the one who invited you to lunch."

"It's the least I can do after causing you such endless suffering." I signal to Ellen on her way back and hand over the bill with my card.

Audrey smiles. "Terrible trauma. The worst." She glances out the window, where Drew Robinson just got out of his truck. He's staring at us, his eyes narrowing. The angles of his face are hard, the scruff on his jaw making him look dangerous. Well, he is dangerous—a blackbelt and former Army Ranger. He practically threw me out of the bar after Audrey yelled at me that night.

He strides toward the restaurant's front door.

"Should I be worried about Drew?" I ask. "He looks lethal."

She rubs the side of her neck, her cheeks high with color. "What? No."

"Were you guys a thing?"

She stares over my shoulder.

I glance behind me as Drew comes through the front door, heading straight for us.

I play it cool when he reaches us despite the fact I want to slowly back away. "Hey, what's up?"

He ignores me, his gaze zeroed in on Audrey. "I was just at the library, and you weren't there."

She gestures airily. "I do take lunch break sometimes. I'm sure you could check out a book with Kathy."

He glances at me and then at her. "What's going on here?"

"Just catching up," I say.

He gives me a steely-eyed look. "I was asking Audrey."

She gazes up at him, an impish look on her face. "What does it look like? I'm having lunch with my ex."

"This is the guy who—" Drew stops himself, his jaw clenching.

My head whips toward Audrey. She told him I was her first? What kind of relationship do these two have?

"The guy who didn't take me to prom," she says and gives me a mock angry look. "I was still mad about that, until Max gave me such a sweet explanation."

Drew's mouth opens and closes. Then he strides off to the back room toward the bar area.

Audrey fusses with the collar of her sweater, pulling it away from her neck.

"What the hell is up with him?" I ask. "You're yanking his chain when I seem to remember you emailed him daily when he was away on his military deployments. What did you call him? It was something like he was better than other guys."

Her cheeks turn bright pink. "Nothing. Shh. What were we talking about before?"

I raise a finger in triumph. "A knight in shining armor."

"I can't believe you remembered that," she mumbles.

"I can't believe you told him I was the guy who—"

She puts a hand over my mouth. "I'm afraid I overshared by email. It's a little embarrassing." She drops her hand and rubs the side of her neck. "A lot embarrassing. I had no idea he remembered that little tidbit. That might explain his hostility toward you."

"You think? And for some reason he's acting like he has a claim on you." I shake my head. "Why would you tell another guy about that in the first place?"

She throws her hands up. "Because I stupidly told him everything like I was writing in my diary. Can we go?" She stands.

I stand and catch Brooke's eye. I jerk my chin at her, ignoring my inconvenient attraction, and walk Audrey out the door.

"Let's go stand by your truck for a moment to chat in private," Audrey says.

Weird. I thought we were just chatting mostly in private. Is there more she has to say to me? Secret-confession type stuff? I walk over with her, a little uneasy.

"Max," she says softly.

I lean down closer to hear, belatedly realizing the height of my truck hides us from view. I parked in the far end of the lot away from the windows, and it's only trees behind us. Is she hoping for something physical? "Yeah?"

"I forgive you."

"Okay. That's good."

"And I'll be honest, I have fond memories of our time together. And it's been *so long* since I met a decent guy. You're decent."

My heart kicks harder. Is she asking me to hook up with her? I can read between the lines with her. *Fond memories. Been so long.*

Then I remember her biological clock. I really don't know what she's driving at with the two of us. We did have something good once.

"What're you thinking?" I ask.

"I'm thinking I'd like you to kiss me."

"And then?"

"Then we'll see."

I hesitate. "What about your biological clock?"

She waves that away. "I'm over it. Let's just—"

I kiss her, a swift kiss. She throws her arms around my neck and kisses me back, a real kiss that's deeper, yet somehow not more exciting.

She pulls away and puts her fingers to her lips.

I stare at her, a little tense as I wait to see if she came to the same conclusion I did—we're ancient history with no future. I don't want to hurt her feelings, but there was nothing there on my end.

She drops her hand, looking disappointed. "It wasn't the same."

The tension drains from me. I know what she means. It felt comfortable and familiar, not exciting. "It's kind of like when you find an old T-shirt you loved and try it on again."

"A soft memory of the past."

"Yeah, familiar."

She hugs me. "We should be friends again, Max. Don't be a stranger. I promise not to traumatize you and call you names again."

I put a hand on top of her head in a gesture of affection I

use on my sister and honorary sister, Sloane. "Sure thing. Now go back inside and ask your knight in shining armor, who apparently already knows everything about you, to kiss you and see what's up between the two of you."

She pushes my hand off her head. "Yeah, that's not happening. He sees me as the young girl with gushing emails full of triple exclamation points and emojis. Before you and I had a thing, I had a huge unrequited crush on him. He doesn't take me seriously, trust me. He'll always see me like a puppy-eyed little sister."

"He looked damn serious when he stopped by our table. Maybe he likes that you called him a knight in shining armor."

"I never told *him* that! Anyway, he's just protective of me because I spent so much time at his house when I was a kid hanging with Sydney." That's Drew's younger sister. She gives my arm a squeeze. "Thanks for humoring an old ex."

"My pleasure."

She walks down the street, probably heading back to work at the library.

I climb into my truck. Guess Audrey can finally move on from any old wound she had from our thing. And I'm out of the running as a husband and dad after that uninspired kiss. The thing is, I know Audrey. She might pretend the whole family thing's not at the front of her mind, but it's what's in her heart.

Anyway, I dodged a bullet there.

5

I dig down, putting my back into lifting the remaining crumbling concrete from the winding path at the back of the Bell estate's main house. Thankfully, the snow melted enough for us to resume work here. We're putting in large stone tiles to replace the concrete. It'll look classier. The Bell estate used to be privately owned by a family, but now it's used primarily for wedding receptions, banquets, and other formal occasions.

I wipe the sweat from my brow. We'll refresh the plantings along the front drive and along the patio after this, trim back some of the overgrown shrubbery along the side of the property, and that's it. Job wrapped with nothing on the horizon but mowing and maintenance. It's been a week, and I haven't heard back from Brooke about the landscaping work for the inn. I glance around at the crew hard at work, a sinking feeling in my gut. Pete, the real estate guy, has three interested clients stopping by my house this weekend. He says it's a good sign to have interest only a few days after posting the listing. If only I could share his enthusiasm.

My phone rings, and I pull it from my back jeans pocket. Brooke. My heart kicks up. Could this be the news I'm hoping for?

I answer with a professional tone. "Max Bellamy."

"Hi, Max, it's Brooke. You got the job. We'd love to hire you to do the landscaping for the inn."

I pump a fist with a silent *yeah*! Adrenaline fires through me, making me feel like I could run a marathon. This could mean I get to keep my house! First I need to find out how much of my plan she's willing to do. That's an in-person conversation in case she needs some convincing. I know the limitations of charm over the phone.

"Thanks, Brooke. I'll stop by for a quick survey and some measurements." *And get the contract signed with your deposit.* "I'll bring the paperwork too. Is now a good time?"

"Are you sure you want to leave in the middle of the workday? We can meet tonight for the paperwork."

"It's no problem. Thanks again. Bye." I hang up and set my shovel against the house. "Harry!" I yell, already on the move. "I need to meet a client. Can you take over here?"

I don't wait around for his answer as I jog to my truck parked in the side lot. I can't help my wide smile. About damn time something good happened. My mind races ahead to having the inn featured in my online portfolio and all the big new clients that could follow. I won't have to sell the house; my brother will be fine; everything will work out. *Yes, yes, yes!*

It's a five-minute drive, and I push the speed the whole way there. I park on the street and spot Brooke walking toward the front yard. Her hands are on her hips, and she's smiling at me.

I get out of the truck and fight the urge to hug her and swing her around. I'm just so happy I won the project. "Hey!"

"That was fast!"

I attempt a shrug, but I'm so wired with adrenaline, it probably looks like a twitch. "I was working on the Bell estate five minutes from here." I close the distance and offer my hand. "Thanks so much for the business. This place is really going to shine."

She shakes my hand with a quick clasp, her green eyes sparkling. "I can tell you're excited for the work."

"Damn—I mean *darn* right."

She laughs. "I work with construction workers. Don't worry about prettying up your language on my account."

"Good to know."

"Come on, we can sit on the front steps to sign the contract. I have my checkbook in my purse." She pats her small cross-body purse. She turns and heads for the steps.

I barely resist smacking my forehead. I forgot the contract in my excitement. It's back at my place. So much for cool professional. "I need to make a quick stop back at the office for the contract." At least "office" sounds professional, even though my office is just the kitchen table.

She turns and smiles, saying in a teasing voice, "Let me guess, you were so excited you dropped your grip on what-ever tool you had in hand—" she tilts her head "—weed whacker? And then drove like a man possessed all the way over here."

Heat creeps up my neck. Substitute shovel for weed whacker and she's eerily close. "Can't help being enthusiastic when I know what this place can become. And don't forget I'm a third-generation Summerdale resident. I want this to succeed for the good of the community. And for you and Paige too, of course. Are we going forward with the full plan?" I'm babbling in my excitement.

She smiles. "Yes to the full plan."

My hands come up to hug her in my excitement, and I quickly drop them. "Yes," I echo, smiling like a maniac, over-joyed by the last-minute miracle. *Hold off, eager city dwellers, my house is not going to the highest bidder.* As long as I stay on schedule here, I can get Liam the money he needs. I have to execute this plan perfectly and on time. "I can't wait to get started."

"Your enthusiasm for the project is part of why we hired you. Just walk on in when you get back, and find me."

I give her a two-finger salute, immediately feel embar-rassed by the gesture, and force myself to walk at a sedate pace back to my truck.

Then I hit the accelerator and race home.

~

One week later, I've got the materials I need to get started at the inn. I brought two crew members to join me there, leaving one behind on the Bell estate, and one guy for mowing and maintenance on existing clients. The snow's melted, and it's the beginning of my busiest season. We're working on hard-scaping and excavating first, starting in the back of the property to stay out of the way of the construction crew coming in and out the front door.

Our first project is a new back patio with lighting. I also had the idea to put in a few upright supports to string white twinkle lights around the perimeter. Figured guests with dogs would like to hang outside a lot, day and night.

I spot Brooke pacing in the distance. This is only my second day here, but she does this frequently, looking agitated. I'm guessing things aren't going as smoothly on the interior work as she'd like. I keep quiet, letting her see us hard at work, everything on schedule out here. I'm grateful for the signed contract and ten percent deposit. I get the next installment at the one-quarter mark, half, three-quarters, and then at completion. If I had the budget to hire more crew, I could get there faster, but it's just not feasible.

Unfortunately, I couldn't give my brother the deposit money. I had to use that for the materials we need. I'm estimating six weeks to completion. I'm hoping to get to the halfway mark ahead of schedule, get the next payment, and pull my house from the market. I had one lowball offer on the house so far, and I countered with a price above asking. The buyer backed out, which is fine by me.

One of my crew guys, Dave, approaches, a grim look on his face. He's in his thirties, already bald, wearing a Bellamy Landscapes cap. I give out T-shirts and caps, as well as dust masks for when we need to cut stone. Safety first.

I jerk my chin. "What's up?"

He takes off his cap and runs a hand over his head. "Hit some big boulders over in the dog play area. I'm going to need an excavator, or we could shift the dog area to the side, but we could run into the same problem over there."

The dog play area is at the far edge of the property near the tree line. Not too surprising there would be boulders. The previous farmers probably cleared the rocks from the open grassy area that was once farmland. Boulders are common in our area. Brooke and Paige chose the spot by the woods so the noise of the dogs wouldn't bother neighbors.

"All right," I say. "Let me go talk to Brooke and Paige and see what they want to do."

"You got it." He wanders over to the patio area I've been excavating and takes a water from the insulated cooler.

I walk around to the front of the house. Brooke told me she and Paige overlap on-site on Thursday and part of Friday. It's late Friday morning, so hopefully Paige is still here. I'd rather not wait until Monday for them to make a decision together. Need to keep the work moving at a brisk pace.

I step through the unlocked front door and into the noise of construction. There's guys in the living room patching up hardwood floor, crew in the kitchen installing cabinets, and more noise out past the den to the left of the staircase. I don't see the sisters in the living room or kitchen area, so I make my way to the den.

There's a gaping hole in the wall just beyond the den, where I guess they're pushing out for more room. Some guys are working just outside the hole. Maybe a bathroom and hallway to the addition? They've got room to add on.

The sisters and Gage, the leader of the crew, are talking in front of a large hearth. Gage is ducking and gesturing inside the chimney. Brooke and Paige look agitated. Maybe not the best time to approach with a problem.

I back out of the room and sit on the narrow stairs in the front hall for a minute to think. I really can't afford to leave things hanging on my work either. Paige will probably leave soon for the city.

A saw dies down, and I hear the sisters' heated discussion. Gage walks right past me on his way to his crew, not noticing me on the stairs.

"He said we *have* to rebuild the chimney and put in a liner," Brooke says. "He's right. That's the building code." I recognize her voice because it's higher than Paige's.

"Or we could close it off and not use it," Paige says. "I like that option."

"We can't *not* have it," Brooke says. "It's part of the historic charm. People will gather in the den and enjoy a cozy fire."

"Okay, then where do you suggest we get the money? We're already over budget from the mold remediation and dealing with asbestos ceilings in the addition."

Silence.

Please don't say cut back on the landscaping project.

Paige continues. "I got it. What if we downgrade the kitchen interior. Instead of—"

"Can't. Everything's already purchased."

"We could return stuff."

"No, the kitchen is important."

"Okay, but we already have a fireplace in the living room. We don't absolutely *need* the den fireplace."

"Paige, we're going to have a lot of guests year-round, and we need plenty of spaces for them to feel comfortable. Think of the cooler nights of fall and winter, guests gathering with warm cider or cocoa around a crackling fire." That does sound good.

"That's optimistic of you to think we'll have guests year-round."

"Of course I'm optimistic! Do you think I went into this thinking it would fail?"

"No, I just thought we'd have a busy spring-summer season and a slow fall-winter. That's what my research showed was typical for B&Bs."

"Not ours."

A pause.

Welp, I've been eavesdropping too long to leave now.

Brooke again. "We could sell your engagement ring. I mean, if you're okay with that."

Ouch. Sounds like Paige had a broken engagement.

"No more anti-man shield," Paige says softly.

"You always said one day you'd want to sell."

Silence.

Paige speaks in a tight voice. "They'll probably take the diamond off its setting to sell, and then it wouldn't even look like the same ring." A pause. "What do I care? It's not like Noah and I are picking up where we left off, even if he is back in New York."

"That's the spirit. Screw Noah. He bailed, and he doesn't deserve you hanging on to any part of him. Seriously, who bails the week before the wedding? On top of emotional suffering, you were out the cost of your wedding gown, the deposit—"

"Don't remind me." And then softer, she says, "Can you take care of selling it?"

"No problem. And whatever we get goes straight into fixing the fireplace, agreed?"

"It's a two-carat diamond with good clarity," Paige says in a choked voice. "We might even have extra."

There's a moment of quiet. I stand and peek over. They're hugging.

Brooke takes off *her* engagement ring and tucks it in her purse. *What!* "It was callous of me to wear it in front of you."

Paige wipes her eyes. "No, it was for a good cause. You had a bad run with guys for way too long."

Hold on. Brooke's wearing Paige's old engagement ring just to keep guys away? That's her anti-man shield? Well, it worked on me.

Brooke is single.

My gaze eats her up from her glossy brown hair to her snug cotton shirt and jeans. *Want.*

I back away and run into Gage. "Crap. Sorry."

"No problem."

He heads past me. Paige darts out the front door.

Is it safe to ask Brooke about the boulder problem? Well, she did find a solution to her fireplace problem.

I round the corner just as Brooke does. She jumps back, her hand on her chest. "You scared me!"

"Sorry. I just ran into Gage too. Hard not to be in the way here. You got a minute to step outside? We're having an issue with the placement of the dog play area."

"Great. Another issue." She gestures toward the front door. "Okay, let's go. Lay it on me."

I turn and head out as she mutters, "This is my life now, one problem after another."

As soon as we're outside, I reassure her. "This is a fixable one, I'm sure. I just need your input." I look around. Shit. "Did Paige leave for the city?" She sells real estate part-time Friday through Sunday.

"Yeah, it's okay. I can deal with this and get back to her if it's major."

I sure hope she signs off today so we can move forward. When we get to the site, I point out the boulders. They really are huge, flat and wide, and who knows how deep they go. I took Dave at his word. He's been with me for nine years now and knows his stuff.

"So, two options," I say. "We can bring in heavy-duty equipment to excavate the boulders, or we can shift the dog area to the side, but we risk more boulders. It's likely the previous owners didn't bother clearing rock along the tree line."

She looks around and points to the side yard. "There. That should be okay for the dog play area."

"What about your neighbor?"

"There's still sixty feet between the properties. The other side is thirty feet to the neighbor, so this is the best option. Problem solved." She wipes her hands together like she's getting rid of the problem. I can't help but notice the lack of sparkling diamond on her finger. How bad was her experience with guys if she felt the need to pretend to be engaged?

I suddenly want to show her we're not all bad. "How's the renovation going?"

She jams a hand in her hair and then smooths it back, tossing her hair over her shoulder. "It's going."

"That good?"

She musters a smile. "I admit I'm more stressed than I thought I'd be. It's my money and my business on the line."

"Sure, it's personal. That'll just make you work harder. I'm sure in the end it'll be a success."

"I appreciate your vote of confidence."

"Happy to help." And then I can't resist. "I'm sure your fiancé's a big support too." I look at her bare ring finger. "Or maybe not."

She lets out a laugh I immediately peg as fake. "Just having the ring cleaned, but yes. Big support. See ya."

I bite back a smile as she hurries away. I wonder how long she'll pretend she's engaged before admitting the truth. I'm going to have fun with this.

6

Max

I looked forward to this Thursday more than I'd like to admit, knowing Brooke would be back at the inn. I haven't seen her yet, but she comes out to the back of the property frequently when she's stressed. I checked in with Sloane, my closest friend, about the fake engagement since she's part of the girl posse now. I figured she could tell me if the fake engagement is an indicator something's seriously off with Brooke or this is just business as usual for single women. It's the first time I've encountered it, but who knows? There could've been other women doing the same thing, and I just didn't know about it. At any rate, according to Sloane's girl posse, the fake engagement isn't as rare as I thought. Sloane says it's right up there with the fake boyfriend to keep guys away. Are there that many crummy guys in the world that women have to go to such lengths? I hope my sister isn't dealing with a lot of jerks, though knowing Skylar, she'd fix them up as best she could and send them on their way.

I take a break from working on the patio and gaze out into the yard. The dog play area is marked out and cleared for the ground covering, an artificial turf that drains. It'll be fenced in too. We have to wait on that because of the public hearing. Thankfully, the rest of my landscaping plan was no problem.

Dave and I are making great progress on the patio. It was slow going with just me before. I'm hoping to collect the next payment installment when we finish here.

Brooke appears in the yard, carrying a laptop case over her shoulder. I go back to work, subtly checking her out. She grabs a folding chair I brought and sets it a distance away in the grass. It's a mild day. She's wearing a maroon down jacket, jeans, and boots. No gloves. Nothing sparkling from her finger. Her long brown hair is up in a messy bun, over-sized dark sunglasses shielding her pretty green eyes.

"New home office?" I call.

She looks over and waves. "Yeah, I couldn't take a minute more of working from my car. Not conducive to releasing stress when you feel cooped up."

I walk over, curious. "More problems with the renovation?"

She grimaces. "The wrong bathroom tile was delivered, and the stuff I want is on back order for six weeks, the addition has crumpled-up newspaper for insulation, so we have to replace that with something more substantial, and my boss expects me to pull my weight at my paying job. That's what I'm attempting now. Otherwise, he's going to think this two days a week of remote work was a bad idea and pull me back to the office."

"I can't imagine working two full-time jobs."

She sighs. "I couldn't afford to give up my paycheck before income starts coming in here, and it's a safety net, you know? If the worst-case scenario I don't dare say out loud about this place happens, I still have a backup." She holds up a palm. "Let's not go there. Anyway, it's only for two more months, fingers crossed." She looks at her laptop. "Could you be any slower!" she yells at it.

"Sounds like you're stretched pretty thin."

She jabs a key on the laptop multiple times. "Like a thread."

My dirty mind immediately thinks massage could help or, better yet, sex as a stress reliever, but I can't say that. She's my best client, signing my paychecks.

"Oh, great," she says flatly. "My program crashed. Let's try this again." She rolls her shoulders. "I desperately need a massage. My shoulders and neck are so tight."

Look at that. We think along the same lines.

"Seems like something your fiancé could help with," I say casually.

She opens her mouth and shuts it with a snap. "I'll mention it to him when I see him next."

"Must be tough to be long distance. You're here Thursday to Sunday. No weekends together."

She gives me a close-lipped smile. "We manage."

I give her my most charming smile, enjoying subtly teasing her about her fake fiancé. Hey, if I can't make a move on my employer, at least I can have a little fun with her. "Back to work for me. The patio's coming along nicely. Stop by and check it out when you get a chance."

"Will do." She glares at her laptop and shakes it. "I need a new laptop."

I go back to work. Not my field of expertise.

She calls over to me, "I appreciate you being so low maintenance and on schedule. Thank you!"

I turn back. "You're welcome. That's my goal. Make it easy for my clients."

She smiles, a genuine smile that warms my chest, before going back to her laptop. I find myself whistling when I get back to work.

∿

Just as we're packing up for the day, Brooke stops by with Paige to check out the patio. It's looking good. I pulled both Harry and Dave in here to accelerate our progress. We're getting behind on local clients' spring cleanups and mowing, but I have to prioritize our biggest client. All we need to do is one more corner area of the patio and then fill in the spaces between the large bluestone tiles with fine sand. Next will be the surrounding patio plantings and lighting. It's the last day of March, and the sun hasn't set yet, so the sisters can get a good look at our work.

"Wow," Paige says. "I love it. I can picture people gathered around a firepit in cushy chairs. Maybe a few chaise lounges off to the side."

"S'mores for the guests," Brooke says.

"Yes!" Paige cracks a rare beaming smile. "I'd rather work out here than in the chaos of the interior. Geez, I never realized how noisy power tools are inside a house."

"I'll keep up with the outdoor supervision," Brooke says quickly, meeting my eyes with a smile. "It's my stress reliever."

I'd love to be your stress reliever, beautiful.

Paige looks at me and then back to Brooke. "Max is your stress reliever?"

Shit. I must've been too obvious in my lust for Brooke. Wait, does Brooke like hanging with me as much as I like hanging with her?

"No!" Brooke exclaims. "That's not what I meant at all."

I head to the far side of the patio, folding up chairs and setting them against my cooler. Not getting involved in the sisterly discussion on this topic. Just doing my job.

Brooke continues. "I meant just being outdoors relieves stress."

The sisters get into a heated whispered discussion. I'd love to leave, but I need to be sure they know my payment is due for completing the first part of the job. Paige's voice rises in agitation enough for me to hear, "Wouldn't want you getting involved with someone we're paying."

She catches my eye and must realize I heard because then she says, "Sorry. We should've had this conversation later in private. You understand about keeping things professional on the job."

I hold up my palms. "No problem. Besides, Brooke's fiancé wouldn't be happy about that."

Paige's head whips toward Brooke's. A silent communication passes between them in a flash. "Right," Paige says. "Nigel wouldn't be happy about that."

Brooke lets out a choked sound.

"Nigel?" I ask, walking over to them. "Sounds like an old British servant."

"He's Irish, if you must know," Brooke retorts. "And he travels back and forth a lot. Anyway, let's get back to the real work here. I saw the patio lighting came in."

Unlike the fake work you put into your fake-fiancé story.

I let her off the hook. "Yup, we'll do that last. I'll dig to make room for the wiring and posts. I have an electrician who'll come in and wire it up. He's already filed for the permit, and he'll deal with the town inspector to get clearance once it's installed."

"I didn't even think of permits for the outdoors," Brooke says, rubbing her forehead. "Why didn't I think of that? We always need permits at my work for the exterior."

"Because you're stretched too thin," I offer. "Don't worry about anything out here. I've got it handled."

Paige puts her hands on her hips. "I'm going to order patio furniture. Then we'll have a nice place to sit outdoors on break."

"Maybe hold off on that," Brooke says under her breath.

They exchange another quick look. I'm guessing it's not in the budget. Cash flow could be tight. I'd better get in my paycheck before it vanishes.

"We'll be wrapping up the patio tomorrow," I say. "Then it's just waiting on the electrician. With the dog play area laid out and the patio, that's the first quarter of the plan wrapped up, like we discussed. First payment is due. I need to keep paying the crew and purchase supplies." *And save my home.*

"Yes," Brooke says. "I'll have your check ready tomorrow after I do a final inspection of your work."

I'd hoped to get it today, but at least she agrees we've finished the first quarter of the plan. I let out a breath. "Fantastic. I'll get started on the koi pond with Dave on Monday. Then it's the vegetable garden and new plantings around back and front. I'm optimistic to finish ahead of schedule."

Brooke throws her hands in the air. "Max, I could kiss you! That is music to this stressed-out architect's ears."

I step closer, drawn in. "Anything I can do to lower your stress level, I'm happy to do."

Our eyes lock, a tension suddenly vibrating between us. *She wants me.* Maybe after I finish the job…

"I'm calling it a day!" Paige says loudly.

Brooke startles and takes a step back, blinking like she's dazed. I kinda know how she feels. There's something real intense when we get up close like that. I forgot Paige was here.

"I'll see you back at Wyatt's," Paige says to Brooke. She turns to me. "Bye, Max. Great work."

"I'll go with you," Brooke says, grabbing Paige's arm.

I watch as they walk off together. Brooke looks at me over her shoulder, a hint of longing in her eyes before turning away.

Now I'm even more eager to finish the job here. Get that final paycheck and make a move on Brooke, free and clear. It's not unprofessional to lust for your client when it's a short-term gig, right?

Brooke

I meet up with Max at the end of the day on Friday. His check is tucked in my pocket. I took a peek at the patio from an upstairs bedroom earlier this afternoon, and from a distance it looks fantastic. I'm glad we added it. He made a good point about guests needing plenty of places to hang outside with their dogs. There's also going to be a seating area by the pond. I'll probably use it as my Zen garden while renovations finish up. I could sure use some Zen. Thanks to numerous issues, we're over budget and three days behind schedule. Every day behind can easily snowball into further delays if we can't get a needed contractor in on time. It's a lot to juggle. And, dammit, I really want this to work.

I walk around the side of the house for the final inspection out back. Max and Dave are cleaning up in their matching navy Bellamy Landscape long-sleeve shirts, sweeping sand

and topsoil off the tile. The plantings are in just below the existing deck and along the side of the patio. Medium-sized ferns that Max says will grow into large leaves. Max is the bright spot in the chaos of this renovation. Always quick with a smile or encouraging words. And he follows through with what he says he's going to do. A man with integrity.

Not that I'm thinking of anything beyond the strictly professional. Can't afford the distraction, and then there's *Nigel*. I could've killed Paige for thinking up such an old-fashioned name. Why couldn't he have been an Ethan or, better yet, something hunky like Jake? A fake-fiancé Jake could be a muscled stud with serious stamina. Nigel not so much.

Anyway, Max is with Audrey. I admit to a pang of jealousy seeing them look so cozy at lunch at The Horseman Inn a few weeks ago. Ridiculous, I know. I have no claim on him. Kayla told me they were deeply in love in high school, and she also said Audrey has been looking for a guy to get serious with for a long time. I like Audrey, a sweet, quiet woman. She's the town librarian.

Although…she doesn't quite fit the type I thought Max would go for. I pictured him with someone more like him— outgoing with a playful sense of humor. Am I describing myself when I'm not stressed to the max? Ha. Max. And maybe.

Just then Max catches my eye and smiles. Warmth spreads through me. It seemed like he was being a little flirty with me yesterday. I stifle a sigh. Isn't that always the way? I attract the cheater guys. It's entirely possible he has integrity at work and none where it concerns women.

He strides over to me and pushes his sunglasses to the top of his head. "Ready to check out your outdoor oasis?"

I nod. "I took a peek from upstairs earlier, but let's see it up close."

He gestures for me to go ahead.

I walk the four corners of the square patio, inspecting the tile work and taking a few pictures to show Paige. I'm really happy with the way it turned out. I follow the new stone path along the back of the house. It ends at the paved driveway.

He appears on the path. "We'll have matching bluestone stepping-stones at the front of the house once your construction crew is done coming in and out the front door. The whole outdoor aesthetic will feel like it flows together."

I close the distance. "Outdoor *aesthetic*, huh? I like it."

"Oh, I know all the beauty words." He leans close, speaking in a conspiratorial tone. "My little sister can talk your ear off."

"And you must be a good big brother to listen."

"No choice in our tiny house growing up." He smiles, and crinkles form at the corners of his blue eyes. So endearing, like he's a man who finds the joy in life. "I love her, don't get me wrong. And she adores me. Just ask her."

"Always a good sign when a guy has an adoring little sister."

"Yeah?" There's a hint of flirtation in his voice.

I remind myself not to get too close. He's seeing Audrey, and I'm paying him. I pull the check from my back jeans pocket. "Here you go."

He doesn't glance at the number, just tucks it into his pocket. "Thank you very much."

We turn and walk back toward the patio.

"Are you short on budget for patio furniture?" he asks. "I could bring over a few chaise lounges from my place. Nothing fancy, but if you and Paige wanted something comfortable when you need a break from the noise inside the house or for you to do your remote work in peace, just let me know."

I turn, warmed by his gesture. "That would be great. We do have the budget for patio furniture, but I'm holding off for a bit. It's just that Paige is used to staging apartments and condos in the city in a sleek modern style. I don't think that fits the *aesthetic* we're going for here." He grins at *aesthetic* like I hoped. "I want to review her choices before she orders anything, and I just don't have time to do it on the two days we're both here in person."

"My sister—the one who adores me—" he winks "—is an interior designer. She went to college for it too and passed the national certification exam. She could be a good addition to your team. She works for a high-end firm in Greenwich, Connecticut, but I'm sure she'd love the chance to do a solo project. She could be a buffer between you and Paige, take the heat off. That way it's just you two discussing options with her rather than arguing with each other."

I can tell he's proud of his sister. So sweet. He makes a good point about the buffer helping to tone down the bickering. I've worked with interior designers before and, while they're not cheap, they often offset their fees with discounts on the furniture and interior decorations through their wholesale connections.

"Couldn't hurt to talk to her," I say.

He pulls out his phone. "Great. Her name is Skylar. She's perpetually sunny. I'm sure you'll love her." He sends her contact info to my phone. "She's young too, so she won't be as expensive as more experienced designers."

"How young?"

"Four years younger than me. Just turned twenty-five."

Okay, so she has at least three years' experience, *and* she's certified with a degree. I'm willing to give her a chance.

He texts me the website of where she works. I click over and scan the home page. Elegant, understated homes. Not quite farmhouse inn, but a lot closer than the modern look Paige favors.

I look up at him. "Thanks, Max. Hiring you was the best decision I've made so far."

"Because I'm easy."

I laugh and continue walking the path back to the patio. He follows. "And you do good work."

"Glad to hear it."

I glance at the two folding chairs tucked with his tools on the side of the patio. Dave left, and the house is quiet. Gage and his crew are already heading back to New Jersey. I'd love to just sit on my brand-new patio and chat with Max. Maybe drink some wine and really relax. Too bad I don't have any wine here.

Still, I find myself asking, "You want to sit for a bit? It's nice out."

"Sure, why not?"

"Great!"

His brows lift at my enthusiasm.

My cheeks flush with heat. "It's just that you're the most relaxing person I've ever been around. I could use that right now."

A small smile plays around his lips. "I relax you?"

I nod. "It's your laid-back vibe. And you don't come with any demands."

"I guess that's good. Normally, you're a ball of stress." He goes to unfold the chairs, facing them toward the tree line in the distance. We take our seats.

"Your guests will love it out here," he says.

I take a deep breath and stretch out my legs. I have on a light V-neck pink sweater, which is just right for the mild day. "I love the view. My mom's place in New Jersey has some trees in the yard, but nothing with such a wide-open feeling like this."

"I grew up here, so I sometimes forget how lucky we are to be surrounded by nature. Where're you from in New Jersey?"

"Princeton. My parents were both professors at the university. Dad was a math professor. He, uh, died when I was nine." My voice chokes, and I stare off in the distance, the familiar ache in my chest returning. It never gets any easier to talk about Dad. My life changed overnight with his death. I don't know why I mentioned it, honestly. I usually keep private stuff to myself.

"Sorry to hear it."

I clear my throat. "Thanks. It was unexpected, a heart attack." I take a deep breath, trying to ease the ache in my chest. "Mom's still a history professor. Me, my sisters, and brother all went to Princeton tuition-free because of them." I glance at him, my throat tight.

He gives me a sympathetic look. "That's lucky to go to Princeton tuition-free. You must be really smart."

I incline my head. "My parents always emphasized education, as you can imagine, with two professors as parents. We were lucky to have the opportunity. Paige and I couldn't have bought this place if we were still deep in debt with college loans."

He looks off at the tree line. "My sister's the only one who went to college in our family *with* student loans. My older brother Liam's a farmer in Vermont." He pauses, his brows drawn together in what looks like deep thought.

"So you didn't go to school for landscape design?"

"Self-taught."

"Guess that would've been a good question to ask before I hired you. I suppose it's the kind of job you can learn by doing. So it seems you and your brother are both outdoorsy people, and your sister is more indoors."

"She's an indoor/outdoor cat. We grew up on the lake and spent most of our childhood running around the beach and swimming."

"Oh, that must've been so nice. I love the lake."

"I still live at the house I grew up in right on the lakeshore. After Mom passed, my siblings and I inherited it. Skylar wanted to live in an apartment close to work, and Liam wanted to stay in Vermont. He owns land there. So it's just me."

"I remember you mentioned you lived in one of the original Summerdale cottages that your grandfather helped build."

He smiles. "That's right. Someone was paying attention."

I sit up straighter, sensing an architectural gem. "Can I get a tour of your house?"

He hesitates. "Now?"

"Well, yeah. I mean, only if you think Audrey wouldn't mind me stopping by."

"Audrey?"

"Yeah."

"Why would Audrey care if you stopped by?"

I stiffen. Do I really need to explain how it could look to his girlfriend? Maybe he doesn't care. "Well, if I were your girlfriend, I might like to know if another woman hung out with you at your place."

"Audrey and I are ancient history."

"But I saw you at The Horseman Inn, and you looked very intimate," I blurt. "You were holding hands."

One corner of his mouth lifts. "Spying on me, huh, Brooke? What would Nigel think?"

I wave that away. "He would just think I was curious. So when did you two break up?"

"Eleven years ago."

"Oh. So you stay friendly with your exes? That's nice."

"Not exactly. She shut me out for a long time, and then recently she wanted to, you know, make up."

Realization hits. "She wanted you back."

He grimaces. "We decided we're better off as friends. It was like an old T-shirt, comfortable and familiar, but not exciting the way it was when we dated in high school."

I relax. "Oh, high school. Yeah, I wouldn't want to be with the guy I dated in high school. So can I see your place before the sun sets?"

"Why not." He stands and folds his chair.

I stand too, folding my chair. Excitement races through me purely for architectural reasons. Okay, I haven't been to a guy's place alone in a long time.

And he's single!

Which doesn't matter because it would be completely unprofessional to cross the line when he's on my payroll. Paige made sure I knew that, which I already did. Then of course there's Nigel. If I admit I made up Nigel, Max will think I'm a total weirdo. Maybe he'll even think I'm delusional, constantly making up fake relationships. This is the first time I've ever done it. Paige's engagement ring has been such a convenient way to take a break from men. Kayla's the one who gave me the idea. She wore it before I did for a fake engagement to Adam (her idea and then his idea to continue —a complicated story) and look at them now, living together and engaged for real.

My little sister's getting married before me and Paige.

That's not how it was supposed to go. It should've been in age order: Paige (almost happened), then me, and then Kayla. Not that I begrudge Kayla her happiness. She deserves it. So do I, but life's unfair. I guess I have to take some responsibility for continually being attracted to the wrong kind of man.

"Meet me there," Max says, grabbing both folding chairs. He rattles off the address on Lakeshore Drive.

"I'll help," I say, holding out my arms for the chairs. They're lightweight.

He hands them over. "Thanks."

My heart beats a little faster, my nerve endings alert. I was so wiped out before this, but now I feel energized. I watch as he gathers up tools and a drop cloth, and follow him to his pickup truck.

He loads up the bed of the truck and takes the chairs from me, his hand brushing mine. A zing goes through me at the touch. Our gazes collide for an intense moment before he abruptly turns away, heading for the rest of his stuff.

I walk to my car with a little bounce in my step. An original cottage, a lakeside view, a gorgeous single man. It really doesn't get any better than this as far as a Friday night break. I don't care about professional boundaries at the moment. I need to let off some steam.

7

I park in the street in front of Max's place and take it in. It's humble, a simple wood-sided ranch-style home with a large attic, as well as a walk-out basement. There's a For Sale sign out front. I didn't realize he was moving.

I head around the corner of the house to see the lake. A staircase leads to a wooden deck on the back of the house, which faces the view. I bet that's where Max spends a lot of time. I would.

I return to the front door just as he pulls into the driveway. He parks and gets out, striding over to me.

"You're moving soon?" I ask.

His expression dims. "Just putting out feelers. Not too serious about selling." He unlocks the front door.

I step into a modest living room with hardwood floors and pale-yellow walls. A dark brown leather sofa dominates the space. "If I had the money, I'd buy this place in a heartbeat just for the view."

"Can't beat the view. You want a drink? Water, beer, or milk."

"I'll take a beer."

He smiles, his blue eyes sparkling. "I knew I liked you for a reason. Two beers coming up."

I follow him to a small kitchen with a dining alcove, the

windows of the alcove facing the lake. The kitchen looks like it was updated in the eighties—dark oak cabinets, light beige Formica counters, vinyl flooring.

He hands me an open bottle of Twisted House ale. Sounds interesting.

"Thanks." I take a sip. "Mmm, it's good."

He smiles around the bottle before drinking. "Local brew. They serve it on tap at The Horseman Inn too." He leans against the counter. "I remember you mentioned wanting to take on part-time architecture work on homes once the inn is finished. Still planning on sticking around Summerdale?"

"I hope so. If, no, *when* the inn is a success—" I cross my fingers in the air "—then I'll look for an affordable place to live in town and work part-time at the inn and part-time as a residential architect working for myself."

"So Paige is the full-time innkeeper and you're what?"

"I'll step in when she has time off and pitch in wherever needed."

"Cool. Summerdale will grow on you."

I smile. "Already has. Wyatt's been giving Summerdale the hard sell ever since he discovered it, and Wyatt being Wyatt, he kept inviting us here to visit, hosting parties, and taking us to local events. His goal is to get our entire family to move here."

"Looks like he succeeded."

I hold up a finger. "Mom is the one holdout. She loves her job, and her friends are in New Jersey. But she did say she'd be our first guest at the inn."

His eyes meet mine intently for a long moment. My pulse thrums pleasantly as I hold his gaze. I really like him.

He straightens abruptly and takes a pull on his beer.

"Would it be okay to get a top-to-bottom tour of your place?" I ask with what I hope is a winning smile. Not everyone likes you poking around their house. "It's the architect in me. I want to see how it's constructed."

He sets his beer on the counter, so I do the same. "You got it."

He gestures for me to follow him to a pantry and opens a

wooden door. "Mom measured us against the inside of the pantry here." He points out different lines with the kids' names on them.

"Aww." The amount of nostalgia built into a home that's been in the family for three generations must be overwhelming. Max and Liam are nearly the exact same height by the last line. Skylar's about six inches shorter.

He shuts the pantry door. "You think that's *aww*, Mom's and her older brother's heights are on the doorframe leading to the attic."

"Double *aww*."

He grins and heads through a short hallway to a mudroom with a washer and dryer. There's an exterior door leading to the deck. "The mudroom slash laundry room."

I would've moved the laundry to the basement and made this space more useful with a bench, hooks to hang wet towels, and a spot for shoes. I keep that to myself. It's not like he's hiring me to renovate the space. I go over to the door with a top window and take in the glittering lake surrounded by trees. A few ducks are on the water, but it's otherwise quiet. I turn to him. "I guess when they built the place, they expected lots of wet and muddy people to be coming in this way from the lake."

"Yup," he says, walking back to the kitchen.

I follow. "If I had a lakeside home, I'd build a great room with wall-to-wall windows and patio doors leading out to the deck."

He stops and turns. "That's not how they rolled in the '60s hippy aesthetic. They kept it simple, figuring they'd mostly be outdoors."

We continue the tour of the main living space. I peek into a small bathroom with a white pedestal sink, a white tub with a cheerful tropical fish shower curtain, and aqua shades of penny tiles on the floor before he gestures vaguely beyond it. "Bedroom."

I peek inside the bedroom. Floral wallpaper, hardwood floor. A few boxes. I bet this was his mom's room. I don't mention it since I know she passed. He must've cleared out her belongings.

He gestures across the short hall. "Skylar's room." I peek into a cute room with a twin-size canopy bed with sheer gauzy drapery. There's a mural of a fairy land that takes up an entire wall. He left it intact for her, in case she visited. Sweet. Or maybe he felt weird using a bedroom with fairies on the wall.

"Nice mural," I say.

"Skylar did that when she was ten."

I take another look, surprised. "It's really good."

"She's been an artist her whole life. Now she uses her art to make people's homes beautiful."

"Does she still paint murals?"

"You could ask her. This is the only one I know about. She's renting now, so I doubt she'd paint the walls in her apartment. Last time I was there, she mostly had large black and white photographs from her trip to Kenya on the walls."

I smile. "She sounds like such an interesting person. I can't wait to meet her."

"I'm sure she'd say likewise," he says over his shoulder, heading to the end of the short hallway to another door. He opens it, revealing a staircase to the attic.

"There's the height marks," I say, marveling over them. Such a classic parent move. You'd think with my dad being a math professor, he would've been into measuring us, but he was more the brilliant absentminded professor type.

He heads upstairs, and I follow.

"Liam and I shared a room up here," he says. "Now it's just me."

There's a queen-sized bed under the window, a pair of nightstands, and a dresser with a mirror above it. The bed is covered with a red and blue tartan plaid comforter. Everything nice and neat.

He keeps his distance, standing across the room from me. Is his bedroom giving him ideas? I know I shouldn't think that way, but it's hard not to. It's been so long, and Max is the first guy I felt comfortable with in a while. Not to mention he's gorgeous, sexy, and a hard worker. His family is clearly important to him. All excellent qualities in a guy.

"I'm impressed you made your bed," I say. "You didn't even know you'd have a visitor today."

"Habit. Mom was a stickler for picking up. I get it now with five people crammed into a small house. She couldn't let it turn into a dump. Besides, it set Dad off if he came home from work and it was chaos. Good times."

"Ah." No love lost there.

I turn around and head back down the way we came. He doesn't follow. I wait a few minutes, curious what he's up to. Finally, he appears, holding a white towel.

"Mind if I grab a quick shower? I always do that when I come home after working outdoors all day."

"Sure."

"Go ahead and relax on the deck with your drink, and I'll meet you there."

I give him a little wave and head to the kitchen, grabbing my beer on my way to the deck. There's two beige mesh chairs and a small plastic table. Perfect. I take a seat and let out a breath. This is the life. I can almost forget my giant list of things to do for the inn and my full-time job. My boss, Bill, has really been on top of me, making me check in more on my remote days. I get the feeling he thinks I'm slacking. I'm not, but I've had to shift his work to the weekend sometimes to keep up.

I shake my head. *No thinking about work.* I take a long drink of beer, gazing out at the lake. Before I know it, my beer's gone. I should probably eat something soon. Oh, look! There's a pair of swans swimming out there. Swans mate for life. That is so cool. I want a picture. Shoot, I left my purse on a kitchen chair.

I head back inside and make my way to the kitchen, leaving my empty bottle on the table to be recycled later. I grab my purse and head back the way I came. Just as I reach the mudroom, the pipes clank, probably because the water to the shower turned off. I bet I could tiptoe into the living room and glimpse Max in a towel, heading to the attic bedroom for a change of clothes. Horny much?

I head outside, bemused by my wayward thoughts. One beer and I'm ready for action. I dig out my phone for my swan picture. I can still see them, but they're farther away. Darn it. I zoom in and take the shot. Hopefully, they'll come back this way soon.

Max appears a few minutes later, wearing a black T-shirt and jeans, his hair still wet from the shower and slicked back. His hair looks a shade darker and emphasizes his blue eyes.

"You're so lucky to live here," I say in a breathy voice. He is *breathtaking*.

He takes the chair next to me and sets his beer on the table. "Yeah, even as a kid I felt lucky to have the lake as my playground."

He points out where he liked to fish in the shade of a weeping willow, and where Liam carved his initials in a tree. More ducks swim around, busily pecking underwater for food.

"The swans are back," I whisper, holding up my phone to get another picture. I snap a few as they swim, and then they still, facing each other, their necks forming the shape of a heart. I snap away. I've got to show Kayla these. She'll love the romance of it.

I turn to Max. "They made a heart. Did you know swans mate for life?"

"I did." His voice sounds husky, his eyes soft.

A shiver of anticipation races down my spine. "I could stay out here all night. I bet the stars are so clear away from streetlights."

A smile plays over his lips. *Was I too obvious with my hint that I want to stay?* He jerks his chin toward the lake. "Better view if you're on the beach or out on the lake in a boat."

"Can we do that? Go out on a boat?"

He leans toward me, his eyes intent on mine. "Do you need to check in with Nigel first? He might take it the wrong way if he hears you're going out on a boat with another guy in the dark of night. Could be seen as…I don't know, romantic."

I swallow hard. *Do I admit there is no Nigel and risk being dismissed as a weirdo?*

On the other hand, if I don't admit it, he might think I'm making a romantic move on him while I'm engaged.

And I'm still technically signing his paycheck.

"What time is it in Ireland?" he asks.

My brows draw together in confusion. "Ireland?"

"Didn't you say that's where Nigel is from? You mentioned he travels back and forth a lot." He stretches his long legs out and crosses them at the ankle. "I assume that's why you're not with him tonight."

I clear my throat. "I'm sure even Nigel would understand two friends gazing at the stars. Besides, I need the peace and quiet."

There. I kept it professional. Dammit.

He gives me a knowing look, one corner of his mouth lifting. "Because I relax you," he murmurs.

My pulse races. Not at the moment, but…is there a vibe here? It feels like he's flirting. Not so much with his words, but with the warmth in his eyes and his husky tone. "You have a very laid-back demeanor," I finally say.

He lifts his bottle in agreement. "That's me." He takes a long drink and sets the bottle on the table. "You seem perpetually tense."

I stiffen. He's basically saying I'm uptight. "That's because you've only seen me trying to tackle the most important job of my life! This is not my normal mode." I shake my head. "Everything is far from normal."

"I'm not trying to insult you. Anyone would be tense taking on two jobs, one of which is full of problems where every single one cuts into your personal bottom line."

"Exactly!" I'm relieved he understands. "So, can we sail on your boat?"

He grins. "It's a rowboat, actually, so we can row." He stands and offers his hand.

I place my hand in his as he helps me out of my chair, a

zing of sensation racing up my arm. It's rare I experience such an intense reaction just holding hands. He doesn't let go, his eyes smoldering into mine. My breath hitches.

"I need to blow off some steam," I whisper.

"I bet you do," he murmurs, one finger stroking the inside of my wrist.

I stare at the spot, mesmerized by his long finger on the delicate skin. My pulse seems to jump every time his finger strokes across it.

He lifts my hand to chest level and turns it to stare at my fingers. "No ring. Are things not going well in Nigel land?"

I tuck my ringless hand behind my back and try not to squirm. I can't stand lying anymore, but I can't admit the truth and risk looking like a flake. I swear I had legit reason to ward off men before! Many terrible experiences that left me without any hope of ever finding a decent guy to settle down with. I can't scare away the first guy I've met in a long time whom I really like and feel comfortable with by admitting I took such extreme measures as fabricating an entire fake-fiancé backstory. I don't even remember mentioning Ireland. Maybe we can forget Nigel ever existed? Nigel who?

I look to the sky. "I sure would like to check out those stars from the water."

"Having doubts about Nigel? It's not final until you say 'I do,' and even then there's an escape clause."

Should I fake a breakup with my fake fiancé? No, I'm not that good an actress. My brother Wyatt loves to play poker with me because he can always tell if I have a good or bad hand. Every emotion plays across my face. I'm surprised I haven't given away the fake-fiancé thing already. I guess the ring spoke for itself.

"Need help getting the boat out?" I ask brightly.

His blue eyes sparkle with good humor. "I got it. Sounds like you could use a break to forget about your troubles with Nigel and work."

"Yes! That sounds great."

He points toward the kitchen. "You get the beer, and I'll haul the boat out of the basement. Meet you outside."

I lean back on my elbows in the boat, taking in the shining stars peppered in a dark cloudless sky, the glow of moonlight filtering through the trees. I'm so relaxed now. It's a little cooler out here at night, but Max gave me a thick sweatshirt to wear, which is oversized enough to give me a little cushion to sit on. Max is *awesome*. He did all the rowing with those big powerful shoulders, gave me beer, and even brought a bag of potato chips. Those are long gone. Dinner of chips and beer hit the spot.

His voice cuts through the moonlit night. "You're going to tip us if you keep leaning on the side like that."

I straighten. "Oops. I just wanted to lie back and look at the sky. I guess I could sit in the middle of the boat and lean back on the bench."

"The bottom is a little wet. Just come over here. You can lean on my shoulder."

"Like a friendly chair." *Or is this Max making a move on an almost nonengaged woman? He thinks there's trouble between me and Nigel. No one could fault me for enjoying a kiss under the stars.*

No one would have to know. Not even Nigel.

There's a hint of amusement in his voice. "Sure, I'm friendly. I've only thrown two women overboard."

I laugh. "I hope that was your sister and a cousin or something. Horseplay is fine with them, but I'm not budging if you throw over unsuspecting women."

His voice takes on a dark sinister tone. "Come here, my pretty. Don't be shy. All is going according to my evil plan."

I narrow my eyes, but I'm not sure how well he can see my expression in the moonlight. I can only make out his glittering eyes and the occasional flash of white teeth. "I'm giving you my best slitty-eyed glare that says *don't mess with me*."

"Brr…scary stuff. Now, don't stand. Move slowly and carefully to my bench." He moves sideways, straddling the bench. Now I get how this'll work. I sit in front of him, and we're still balanced on the bench.

"I guess this is why you suggested a life vest," I say, half crouching off my bench and leaning in his direction. "I can swim, but I'd rather not get soaked right now."

He grabs my wrist suddenly, and I gasp in surprise. He draws me the rest of the way toward him, settling me on the bench in front of him.

"Okay, lean back," he says.

I glance over my shoulder. He's shifted away to give me room. I slowly lean back against his chest covered by a thick sweatshirt and rest my head against his shoulder. How is he so warm on a cool spring night? Or maybe I'm the one who's warm. I like this a whole helluva lot. And that's not two beers talking.

I stare at the sky, dazzled once again by the clarity of so many brilliant stars. "It's beautiful."

His voice rumbles in his chest. "It is. I never want to lose this."

I shift to look at him. "Then why did you put the house on the market?"

He tucks a lock of hair behind my ear. "Don't ask," he murmurs.

I'm enthralled, wrapped in a warm cocoon just the two of us out on the water. Do I dare close the distance?

He looks away. "There's those swans in my fishing spot from when I was a kid."

I look over, disappointed. But then he puts his arms around me, and it feels so good to be held I let out a sigh. In the distance, I catch a glimpse of the swans, their white feathers glowing in the soft light. I just want to permanently freeze this moment—being held in Max's warm embrace, the glittering night sky, the water gently lapping against the boat.

I rest my hand on his forearm and then slide my palm down to his hand, resting mine on top of his. I can't even remember the last time a guy held me. Maybe a year ago, I woke up with an ex spooning me, but then it turned out he just wanted round two. I never saw him again. That stung. I thought when Sam spent the night, it meant something. That was just his usual two-for-one-night mode of operation. I push the memory down. I'm enjoying now too much to dwell on my terrible history with men.

Max's other hand rests on top of my head before sliding down to stroke my hair. "You have the softest hair."

"It's so fine. I can never get it to curl. Paige and Kayla have naturally wavy hair. Those genes missed me."

"I like it just the way it is," he says silkily.

I shift at the hint of invitation and stroke my fingers along his bearded jaw. "Your beard is softer than I thought."

He gazes into my eyes.

I impulsively press my lips to his, rewarded instantly with a jolt of sensation. I shift back, and we stare at each other.

This time he kisses me, his hand cupping my jaw, his mouth slanting across mine in a kiss that makes my stomach drop and desire pool between my legs. I'm shocked at my response. I always thought I was slow to warm up.

He breaks the kiss, gazing at me with a serious expression on his face. "As much as I enjoyed that, I'm not messing around with an engaged woman."

"We're breaking up," I say quickly. "It's over with Nile—"

"Nile? I thought it was Nigel."

I still. *Crap*. "It *is* Nigel. Sorry. Too much beer? Kiss me again."

He smiles widely and chucks me under the chin. "I know you made up Nigel."

"What! How do you know that?" I shift so I'm sitting sideways on the bench to look at him. Then I realize I just admitted it. "I mean, what're you talking about?"

He chuckles, a broad smile breaking out in what could only be called maximum male gloating. "I overheard you and Paige talking about selling the ring. Your anti-man shield."

I dip my hand over the side of the boat, scoop some lake water, and splash him just so he'll stop gloating. He splashes me back, and I shriek. The water is cold, and he soaked my head! I scoop as much as I can as fast as I can, getting him back. He gives as good as he gets. Even the thick sweatshirt he gave me is soaked through in minutes.

"Truce!" I yell.

He stops instantly, his hand curling around the back of my neck, pulling me close. He grins. "You look cute soaking wet."

Is he about to toss me overboard?

"So do you," I say, throwing my arms around his neck. If I'm going down, he's going with me.

"I can kiss a single woman." And then he does. A deep long kiss that steals the breath from my lungs. My mind shuts down, and my body ignites, making me forget everything but this—his heat, his taste, an urgent desire that consumes me.

We stay right there, kissing under the stars, for a very long time.

∾

Max

I made it back to the house, even managed to get both of us into dry things and throw stuff in the dryer, but what I haven't managed to do is stop kissing Brooke.

She's straddling my lap on the sofa, wearing my T-shirt and jogging pants, both of which are so loose I've got easy access to her soft skin. She grinds against me, giving us both what we need, and my intense need skyrockets. I fight the urge to pull her under me.

I break the kiss, taking her in. She's breathing faster, her green eyes dilated, cheeks flushed. So fucking sexy.

"What?" she asks in a breathy voice.

I open my mouth to say I don't want to take advantage, but dammit, I do. I grip her hair and kiss her again, drowning in sensation. Her soft curves, silky hair, the heat of her mouth. She smells like flowers. How can she still smell like flowers after I doused her with lake water?

I should stop. My hands slide up her back, no bra. *Wait. Slow it down.*

I lift my head. She grabs the hem of my T-shirt, tugging it up.

"We should hold off," I say hoarsely.

She stares at me, her eyes wide. "Really?"

I grasp for my last bit of willpower. "It's not a good idea for me to mess around with a client."

She pushes her hair out of her face, still looking dazed. "Right." She climbs off my lap and sits next to me. "I guess I got carried away."

"Not that I'm not enjoying…everything."

She stares straight ahead for a long tense moment. "I'll just go." She stands, looking off toward the back of the house. "I'll get my clothes from the dryer."

I grab her wrist before she can walk away. "Just so it's not messy between us, with you being a client."

She keeps her gaze fixed in the distance. "Totally get it. Won't happen again." She pulls away and darts into the mudroom.

I exhale sharply. She seems upset. I'm trying to do the right thing here.

She returns wearing the pink sweater she arrived in, still damp and clinging to her breasts. My hands itch to roam freely along her hourglass shape. I cross my arms in an attempt to keep my hands corralled.

She looks around for her purse and puts the strap over her shoulder. She finally meets my eyes and gives me a tight smile. "Thanks. Tonight was fun. I left your borrowed shirt in there for the wash. So, I'll see you next Thursday when I'm back at work at the inn. And, don't worry, it'll be totally professional between us."

Next Thursday suddenly feels so far away. It's Friday night. I know she's in town Thursday through Sunday. "Do you ever work weekends at the inn?"

Her voice takes on a brusque professional tone. "If I can get a contractor in. Sometimes Gage will send one or two of his crew if I need them, or the occasional electrician, flooring guy, or whoever. Most times I'm there reviewing what's been done and what needs doing. Then I crunch the numbers."

I miss her warmth. "I could put in some work on Saturdays to get ahead of schedule." I've been eager to get ahead of schedule to accelerate payment for Liam's sake and my house, but now I want to finish up fast so Brooke and I can pick up where we left off. I want her more than I've wanted any woman in a very long time. I can't say any of that when she's my best client.

She shrugs, and her purse drops to the floor. She grabs it. "Whatever you want. I'll see you."

"Maybe I'll see you at the inn tomorrow."

She waves airily, her voice high. "Yeah, or next Thursday."

I stand and walk her to the door.

She stops at the door and sighs, looking up at me. "Can we pretend this never happened?"

"Sure."

I push open the door for her, bringing our bodies in close with the movement. We stare at each other for a moment and slam together. I'm not even sure who moved first. I want her so fiercely I pin her against the wall, kissing her like a starving man, my body pressed against hers, aching with need.

She breaks the kiss, breathing hard. "Apologies."

"Forgiven."

I kiss her again, hungry for more. Her hands are all over me. I run my hands down her sides, feeling her heated skin through the damp shirt. I shift to kiss along her neck, letting my teeth scrape against her.

"Max," she gasps out. "Raincheck." She pushes at my chest.

I back off, out of breath and near crazed with lust. I can't remember ever ramping up that fast from a kiss. I run a hand through my hair, trying to calm down. *Right. Professional. Got it.*

Sucks to be responsible. Wait. I'm the irresponsible one. Isn't that what everyone always says? A chip off the old block.

She strokes my beard. "Bye, Max," she says softly.

"Bye." I take in her flushed cheeks, her pink lips, and it takes everything I have not to grab her again.

I shut the door behind her and watch through the window of the door as she gets in her car, and then keep watching until the car is a distant light in the distance.

I walk back to the sofa and flop down. *Fuck.* I screwed up.

If anything goes wrong between us, it'll ruin a much-needed project for not just my business, but for my brother and for saving my family home. What the hell was I thinking?

The scary thing is, if she walked through that door right now, I wouldn't be able to resist temptation. The only solution is to keep my distance as much as possible. We'll pretend like this never happened just like she said.

If only I could get the memory of her mouth on mine, the feel of her in my arms, her floral scent—just everything Brooke—out of my mind. Her bright smiles, her infectious laugh, her direct straightforward way. So many women have a hidden agenda. Brooke is what you see is what you get. I love that.

I miss her already.

8

Brooke

I brought my golden retriever, Scout, with me to the inn today as a buffer between me and Max. In fact, I'm only doing a quick check-in to review progress and meet the potential interior designer, Max's sister, Skylar. It's been six days since I last saw Max, and I've thought about our brief trip to lusty insanity way too much. I crossed a line I shouldn't have crossed, and that will never happen again. It's like it never happened. Just like my engagement. Vanished. *Poor Nigel. He took it hard. Ha-ha.*

Thankfully, everything's moving along nicely on the renovation. The living room walls have been replastered, and the hardwood floor repaired in a few spots. The kitchen is complete too, so it's on to air-conditioning, chimney repair, new bathrooms, updating the bedrooms, and adding adjoining doors to two sets of bedrooms. Last will be the innkeeper's apartment. Paige's apartment is just a large empty room right now. The previous owner used it as a quilting space.

I keep Scout on a short leash and meet up with Paige in our newly renovated kitchen. Scout's enjoying sniffing everything. The stainless-steel appliances still have the clear protective plastic over them. Paige's back is to me as she refills her water bottle from the sink.

"Nice to have running water again," I say.

"The things you never realized you take for granted," she says over her shoulder. She finishes filling up and leans against the counter, taking a drink.

"I'm just here for a short time today."

Her brows lift in question. It's the first time I didn't spend the full day here while I was in town.

I'm saved from explaining why I'm making myself scarce by the doorbell. Scout barks, jerking the leash, eager to run to the door. I give him the quiet command. He whines, but it's much quieter than his bark. His gaze remains fixed on the front door.

"Must be Skylar," I say to Paige, who's on her way to answer it. "The crew would just walk in."

"Or Wyatt."

Our older brother has been bugging us to let him stop by to inspect our progress. We've been trying to hold him off until it's finished. Wyatt means well, but if you give him an "in," he'll take over. He can't help it. It's in his nature to see a problem and step in to fix it. He's probably worse with us than his business associates because he stepped into the man-of-the-house position when Dad died, and firmly believes his three younger sisters are his responsibility. Doesn't matter that we're all adults now. I love him dearly, but…

Here's a classic Wyatt scenario: I recently learned the digital tile he gave me and my sisters for our key rings, so we could find them if they were lost, was also how he kept track of *us* on an app. Tracking his own sisters! I never looked at the app because I hadn't lost my keys. Apparently, Paige kept her digital tile in her nightstand drawer after the first day because she did check the app. She never thought to mention it to me. Even Kayla knew before me and never mentioned it. She'd put her tile on her fiancé's dog's collar in case he was dognapped (long story). Anyway, that's how Wyatt found the dog, using the app that tracked all of our tiles. I'll be thinking twice before accepting a gift from him in the future.

I join Paige and Skylar in the living room. Skylar exclaims over Scout. "Aren't you a beauty?" She pets him and smiles at me. "I just love golden retrievers." She's a pretty brunette, wearing a pink and orange floral tie-wrap shirt with black trousers and heels.

Scout must love her too because he leans against her leg, gazing adoringly up at her. Funny, Scout loves Max too, much more than most people. Something about those Bellamy pheromones or something.

Skylar beams a smile at me and offers her hand. "Sorry, your gorgeous dog distracted me. It's so nice to meet you, Brooke! Max told me you're an *amazing* architect."

I shake her hand, already liking her. "Thanks. Max told me you're an amazing interior designer."

She flips her long brown hair over her shoulder, grinning much like her brother. "Well, I try." She pulls her phone from a leather satchel. "Do you mind if I take pictures while I get the tour? That will help me to plan some fun ideas later."

"I know a lot about decorating," Paige says. "I stage apartments and condos in the city."

I shoot her a look. We agreed that an interior designer could be a help.

Skylar keeps a pleasant expression. "I heard about that. I'm sure you're very good at your job. I'm just here to be the idea person, and if you decide you'd like me to work alongside you, we'll be a team." She turns to me. "You too, Brooke. I love working with clients and figuring out what would really speak to them." She puts a hand over her heart. "It makes me happy to make you happy."

I love her already. Max predicted it. I glance at Paige, who doesn't look convinced.

"Right this way," I say, gesturing for Skylar to follow. "We'll start upstairs since the crew hasn't tackled that part yet. You'll get a peek at the before. That way we can incorporate any ideas you have in the future."

I guide Scout to the steps and let go of his leash so he can race up the stairs.

Skylar *oohs* and *aahs* over every room I show her. She's

loving the house as much as we do. By the time we're back in the living room, even Paige is smiling. Probably helps that Skylar had an idea to make the innkeeper's apartment into an open floor plan, the kind that appeals to Paige's modern style.

The living room is an empty space for now with large windows on two sides, a fireplace, plaster walls, and a cool post and beam ceiling. I can see the olden days in the room, and also how it could be a cozy more modern space with the right furniture and lighting. I'd love to have flowers in vases according to the season. Ooh, I should add flowers to our vegetable garden out back. I'll mention it to Max.

Scout's tuckered out from the excitement of our tour. He's sleeping by my feet now.

Skylar studies the ceiling for a moment and then looks around the floor. "Some footboards would look great in here."

Gage walks in and halts, his gaze locked on Skylar. If you didn't know Gage, you might find that intimidating. He's big with inked arms and has a hard expression with his sharp angular features and scruffy jaw. His expression is usually dialed to *get out of my way, I've got a job to do*.

"Gage, this is Skylar," I say. "She's an interior designer."

She notices him and walks over, a bright sunny smile on her face. She offers her hand. "Nice to meet you. Just taking notes for later."

Gage gives her a quick handshake, his expression stone.

Skylar puts her hands on her hips and looks around the room. "You know what would be fantastic? Lowering the floors to make the height of the room higher. They didn't make older homes with that light spacious feeling they do nowadays."

Ooh, why didn't I think of that? No one cares about a shorter ceiling in the basement. Of course, it *is* a major construction project.

"Did you say lower the floors?" Gage asks tightly.

Skylar smiles. "Yes. To bring in more light and give us the feeling of more space." She walks up to him and puts her hand up near the top of his head. "Look, the ceiling's only a couple of inches from the top of your head. Wouldn't your head like more space?"

Gage stares at her. They're standing toe-to-toe because Skylar hasn't backed away after measuring him, and it seems Gage doesn't want to be the one to back off.

"Yes, right?" she coaxes with a winning smile.

Gage doesn't smile back. "No fucking way. Excuse me, no effing way."

"It could really open the space up," she says blithely, unconcerned by his language. She did grow up with two older brothers. She gives him a once-over. "I'm guessing by your tool belt and your firm opinion that you're in charge of the crew?"

He nods once.

She continues brightly. "I'm so glad we met before the renovation is finished because now we can work together to make any teensy changes that might work better for flow."

"Not in the budget," he says between his teeth. "No time on the schedule."

He's right, though I'm curious how much it would cost. I open my mouth to ask, but it seems I'm not needed here for the *Gage stonewall-Skylar sunny skies* skirmish.

"Schedules change," Skylar says with a nod. "And budgets can be finagled. Add a little here, take away a little there. It's all very workable if we get a little creative."

He scowls. "Who do you think you are?"

She stands taller, her shoulders drawing back. "Skylar Bellamy, interior designer, at your service." She glances at me and Paige. "Well, I hope to be if Paige and Brooke decide to work with me."

Gage relaxes. "Good, you're not actually hired." He strides past her to the kitchen, where he helps himself to water.

Skylar's gaze follows him as she mutters, "Nice meeting you too, Mr. Grumps."

Gage doesn't react, but he must've heard because as he crosses through the room on his way back, he grumbles,

"Miss Perky," just as he passes her. He continues on toward the den.

"I am perky, thank you very much!" Skylar yells after him. "The world needs positive people!"

Paige and I exchange a look. Hmm, not sure if those two should be working together.

Skylar turns to us. "Sorry. I lost my temper for a moment there. Is he always like that?"

"Pretty much," I say.

"Wow," she says. "Just wow. Anyway…" She takes a deep breath, closing her eyes for a moment, and then opens them, a bright smile in place. "I'll work up a plan. I already got your filled-out questionnaires, and now that I've met you and seen the place, I'm excited to work with you both."

"You too," I say.

"I look forward to seeing the plan," Paige says blandly.

"Great! I'm going to stop out back to say hi to Max," Skylar says.

"I'll go with you," I say, sensing an even better buffer than Scout. "I want to check on the pond before I go."

We head out the front door since the new back door is in the construction zone. Scout perks up as soon as we step outside, trotting with his tail up, looking thrilled. He's a happy guy.

I immediately pick out Max, even though his back is to us as he digs for the koi pond. It seems I've memorized the shape of his shoulders and back in his navy Bellamy Landscapes T-shirt. Dave's with him here today, a good-natured guy in his thirties. He's working on clearing a space for the new vegetable garden.

Skylar moves with a half skip-half walk toward him. "Max! My favorite brother in New York!" Her other brother is in Vermont.

He turns, a broad smile on his handsome face. "Sky!"

She runs toward him with a laugh. He gives her a hug that lifts her off her feet, and sets her down, resting his hand on top of her head. She pushes his hand away and smacks his shoulder. He was right. She adores him, and he adores her right back. My heart squeezes at the warm family moment. Max is a good big brother.

Scout takes off unexpectedly, the leash flying from my hand. I rush after him, not wanting him to get lost in the woods at the back of the property.

Oh, he's heading for Max, and Max is distracted by Skylar.

"Max!" I yell. "Watch—"

Scout leaps on him before I can get the words out. Max stumbles back, loses his footing, and lands on his ass in the half-dug pond. Scout stands with his front legs on Max's chest and licks his face.

I rush over and stop short, not wanting to get dirt all over my white sneakers. "Sorry! Scout, come!" I lean forward to snag the leash, but it's out of reach.

"Get off me, you slobbery beast," Max says, pushing Scout away. As he's trying to get up, Scout jumps on him excitedly.

"Scout, off!" I turn to Max, mortified. "I swear I took him to obedience classes. He's usually not like this."

Max hands me the leash, his palms covered in dark soil. "Your dog is a menace."

"Don't say that!" Skylar exclaims. "He's just a big lovey. Aren't you, Scout?"

Scout races over to her, and she crouches down, petting him. At least he didn't jump on her. I don't know what it is about Max that makes Scout so crazy.

Max steps out of the pond, brushing dirt off. He twists to look at his back side. Unfortunately, the dirt is really stuck on him. More like mud actually. What a mess. Scout rushes him in excitement, sniffing his jeans and then bumping his hand for pets. Max obliges, petting him behind the ears. "Dope," he says.

Scout pants happily up at him like he's in love. I'm starting to feel that way myself.

~

The next day is one problem after another. A new bathroom cabinet was damaged upon arrival, a front bedroom window was broken by a bird who flew straight into it—poor bird died on impact—and Gage called out sick, which he never does, so I know it must be bad. He's not sure if it's food poisoning or a stomach virus, so I've been trying to take his place, going over the jobs that need to be done today with the crew, all while Paige keeps sharing what she likes and doesn't like about Skylar's ideas from yesterday. We haven't even seen Skylar's plan yet. Paige is still trying to hang onto her status as superior decorator because of her staging experience. It's not like she went to school for that. Paige majored in economics. She hated working in banking and picked up the real-estate gig.

It's a relief when Paige finally leaves for the city that afternoon. I slip away from the construction noise, heading toward the quiet of the innkeeper's apartment to make some phone calls. My first priority is to source a historic window for our broken window; otherwise it won't match the rest of the house. We could tear out a back window to replace it, but that risks damaging more of the house.

When I arrive in the space, I'm surprised to see an air mattress with a pillow and Paige's yellow polka-dotted comforter. Did she spend the night here? I heard her and Wyatt arguing late last night. She'll often go out for air when she's mad. She must've come here. I thought she just got to the inn early this morning. I glance around and don't see anything else she left. Maybe she just wanted a place to crash when she needs space from Wyatt. They're closest in age of us siblings, and Paige doesn't put up with Wyatt's overprotectiveness or his penchant for butting in. Doesn't stop him, though.

I make my calls to everyone I can think of who might have access to a historic window, including a woman I work with at the office, and it's a dead end. I'll circle back to that. My shoulders get tenser and tenser as I pace the room, talking to the bathroom cabinet people, rescheduling the sink and counter guy, and then following up with my boss, Bill. He's not happy with how long it takes me to get back to him on my remote days. Not for nothing but I've busted my ass at his firm for the last four years. You'd think he could give me a little slack for not being at his beck and call two days a week. I do return all calls and emails by the end of the workday.

I shove my phone in my purse, not wanting to look at all the notifications, messages, and missed calls. I just need a break. I wander over to the rear window and see Max working on the koi pond, setting in a liner. I left Scout at home today after his embarrassing incident knocking Max into the mud of the pond. Max was a trooper and said he didn't want to lose time on the job, so he didn't even go home to change. He assured me he had a towel in the car to sit on for the drive home.

Dave's working on a waterfall feature nearby, but my gaze returns to Max, remembering last Friday and how we took a moonlit boat ride, the way he held me, the way he kissed me. I don't know quite what it is about him. He relaxes me just by being himself, which makes me feel safe. I don't think I've ever felt safe with a guy before. At the same time, he excites me.

Don't go there! With all the stress piling up on me, I have very little willpower left to deal with denying temptation.

I head back downstairs to the chaos of the crew still hard at work, and make my way to the kitchen. It's not fully operational. Everything's in place, covered protectively with tarps. I usually bake chocolate-chip cookies to destress—it's the warm smell of chocolate, butter and sugar, the gooey goodness of biting into a fresh-baked cookie that does it for me every time. I can't bake here, and I don't have the time anyway. My second shift starts right after this one, working on my actual job. My shoulders tense just thinking about it.

I make my way outside, telling myself I'm just going to check on Max's progress. I can't keep my distance from someone who works for me, right? And I always relax when I'm around him.

What if Max was my stress reliever? A casual, no-strings stress reliever. My heart skips a beat at the thought.

I arrive at the back patio just as Max takes a chilled bottled water from a cooler there. My pulse skitters, taking in his gorgeous self. Those wide shoulders and muscular arms. Big capable hands.

One corner of his mouth lifts as he peers over my shoulder. "No Scout to pounce on me today?"

I smile sheepishly. "No Scout. I don't know why he gets so excited over you. It's a little embarrassing."

He twists off the cap and takes a drink of water. "I'm an exciting guy."

I step closer, half inclined to take a page from Scout's book and pounce on him. "How so?"

"He saw me digging in the dirt. That's right up there on a dog's favorite things list. He wanted to join the fun."

"Yes, but he's jumped on you plenty when there was no dirt around."

He grins, his blue eyes sparkling devilishly. *Want.* "The bearded wonder." I called him that before.

"You want to get a drink at The Horseman Inn tonight?" I hold my breath, trying to keep a casual expression like it's no big deal.

"How about dinner?"

9

Max

At the end of the day, I turn toward the house to find Brooke. We're at the halfway mark in the project, which means the next payment. And I need to firm up our dinner plans. She waves to me from an upstairs window and gestures for me to join her. I go through the new hallway and back staircase to find her in the innkeeper's apartment.

I step into the room and stop short. There's a large mattress on the floor with a girly yellow polka-dotted comforter. Apparently, Brooke wants something more than dinner.

She slowly approaches me, hips swaying, her gaze intent on mine. "Hi."

So many things flash through my mind in that moment—dinner, *sex*, my payment, *sex*, biggest client, *sex*. But what comes out is a slow, "He-e-ey."

She throws herself at me, her lips meeting mine as her arms wrap around my neck. I can't resist. No man could. She's so sexy, her tongue licking into my mouth. I cup her ass and press her against me, the ache nearly unbearable. She moans softly.

She breaks the kiss suddenly and takes off her blue ruffly blouse. My mouth goes dry. She's so beautiful. She yanks my

T-shirt up, and I finish the job. Then she's back in my arms, kissing me passionately. Need like I've never known before roars through me. I can't get enough, kissing her while caressing so much soft skin. I slip the straps of her bra down, find the clasp, and send the bra flying.

Her hands fumble at my jeans' button, and I break the kiss, breathing hard. "Brooke, wait. Are we really going to do this? What about—"

She's already peeling out of her jeans. "It's okay. I'm on the pill."

I rack my brain, trying to come up with the rational argument I thought I had waiting there. Nope. I got nothing. "I'm healthy."

"Me too." She pulls the comforter to the side, lies down, and spreads her legs in invitation. "I once heard that sex is the best stress relief. Max, I could *really* use some relief."

I jolt into action, undoing my jeans and yanking them down with my boxer briefs. "I heard that too."

I'm on her in a flash, the impact of full skin on skin bringing a rush of sensation. I prop myself on my forearms and kiss her tenderly, working hard to slow it down. I want to make it good for her.

"Max," she says softly when I kiss her forehead. I keep going, kissing all over her beautiful face and then the crook of her neck, where she smells like flowers.

I lower myself to her breast, kissing slowly round and round as her nipple forms a rigid point.

"Max," she whispers, "I'm ready."

I suckle her, my other hand caressing the other breast, getting it ready for my attention. Her fingers tunnel through my hair. I glance up. Her head's back, her lips parted as she breathes heavily.

I shift to her other breast, sucking hard. Her hips move restlessly under me, begging for my attention. I shift, sliding my hand between her legs, heading straight for what I think of as the hot button. One touch and women go wild. *There it is.* She gasps, her hips arching off the bed.

"Okay?" I ask, thinking maybe I moved too fast.

She nods vigorously. "It's been way too long for me."

Not a small amount of pride fills my chest. She chose *me*. I must be irresistible.

"Don't look so smug," she says. "This is stress relief."

No strings. No expectations. It's perfect.

I kiss her, still stroking between her legs, feeling her desire build. She moves to my rhythm, making these needy sounds in the back of her throat. My own need skyrockets.

I lift my head, gazing into her eyes. Those green eyes stare back at me, and then they close as she cries out, shuddering with her release. *Yes!*

I can't wait. I thrust inside her, and she gasps, her eyes flying open. She's so tight, unbearably good. I still, giving her a moment.

"Wow," she says. "You feel amazing. My turn." She pushes my shoulders, trying to shift me off her.

I roll to the side and settle her on top. She eases herself in place, letting out a soft moan. Her long hair floats above me in a silky curtain, her body tight and hot. I'm nearly there, and she hasn't even moved yet.

I grab her hips, guiding her to slowly rock.

She doesn't mind, her eyes closing, her head dropping back. "I'm hardly ever on top," she says in a breathy voice. "This is what it's like when you're not overthinking it."

"You're a talker." I wonder what I can get out of her she wouldn't normally say. I stroke her lightly, teasing more pleasure from the hot button I so recently coaxed to orgasm. She's panting now. "Tell me all your dirty fantasies."

"Ah-ah-ah, Max!" She rocks her hips faster and faster, her fingers clutching my shoulders. I fight for control, my own need clawing at me.

Hang on, hang on, hang on.

She goes off with a sharp cry. I grab her hips, surging into her again and again as she makes the sexiest gasps. I let go, an explosion of pleasure rocketing through me. The room dims for a moment, my ears ringing. I collapse, losing my grip on her hips. Sensation floods me even in the aftermath. Hot satiny skin, her silky hair, the floral musky scent in the air.

She kisses me. "Thank you."

I grin. "Thank *you*."

"I usually bake cookies to destress, but this is way better."

I stroke her hair back from her face, a rush of affection going through me. *Cookies*. I could get used to this. Naked time with Brooke, dinnertime with Brooke, talking on a warm night or a cool one or in bed. Just being with her.

"Anytime," I murmur, stroking along her jaw.

"Paige would kill me if she knew about this. Don't tell her. Not that you would. You understand keeping it quiet, right?"

Cold reality creeps in. This could cause a rift between them. And they're signing my paycheck. They already bicker, and if Paige thought Brooke was fooling around on the job…

I lift her off me and set her on the mattress. She immediately cuddles up to my side and pulls the comforter over us. I go stock-still, unsure of the right thing to do here. Forget all those mushy affectionate feelings. That was just afterglow. Pretty sure. Anyway, I should backtrack, say this will never happen again, and get out.

She grabs my arm and puts it around her shoulders, forcing the cuddle. I'm no stranger to the cuddle. I did have a five-year relationship right out of high school, where cuddling was mandatory after sex if I didn't want to deal with a spitting mad woman. Still, isn't this the point where one of us should put up a boundary?

For the sake of no strings.

And professional stuff.

And me getting paid by the person who just gave me the best sex of my life.

I swallow hard, trying to find the right words. I don't want to hurt her feelings. Women can be so emotional after sex.

She rests her head against my shoulder and strokes my chest. Her hand stills over my heart. "Your heart's beating fast. That was awesome, right?"

"Right." She's a talker before and after, and I can't bring myself to leave the warmth of the bed. My fingers idly trace the curve of her shoulder. At some point, one of us has to address the problem with what we just did. It can never happen again.

"You do good work," she says.

My lips curve. I did give her two orgasms. "You're welcome."

She laughs. "I meant on the landscaping stuff. You should raise your rates for commercial projects. You were cheaper than all the other bids we got."

I shift to look at her. "By how much?"

She looks to the ceiling, deep in thought. "Twenty percent."

I stare at the ceiling. "Dammit."

"I'm just telling you for going forward."

"This job is only my second commercial client, and I gave the first one a thirty percent discount in exchange for a discount on catering for the Winterfest ball."

"Well, that sucks."

"No kidding!" I grab her and tickle her. She shrieks, batting at me in between gulps of laughter.

I pin her under me, holding her wrists on either side of her head. "It does suck. Thanks so much for pointing that out."

Her eyes are bright, color flooding her cheeks from all that laughing. Her beauty, just everything about her draws me in. It doesn't hurt that we're fully naked, and I'm on top of her. Desire stirs once again.

"Hey, I didn't have to say anything about your bid," she says. "That was a favor from one friend to another."

Friend. Ha! "Well, my *friend* just gave me the best I've ever had."

She bites her lower lip, her eyes going soft. "Really?"

I release her wrists, regretting admitting that. It's only going to make it harder to keep her at a distance for professional reasons. I look to the side, gathering the strength to leave her.

She throws her arms around my neck, smiling widely. "Me too."

I could drown in that smile. *Resist. Get dressed.* "It can never happen again," I say firmly.

She strokes my beard. "Never." And then she grabs my head and kisses me.

I dive back in for more. This time doesn't count.

Brooke

So *that* happened and now *this*. Max and I are having dinner at The Horseman Inn on what feels like a date. Maybe it's the afterglow talking, but I'm so warm and content. Everything seems brighter in the world. Like I'm just waking up again after a long slumber. Is it because I finally broke my dry spell, or is there something more?

I take a bite of spinach, telling myself to keep to my first instinct. Sex as stress relief, nothing more. I never do casual, and I feel so good right now. Normally, I'd be overthinking it or worrying he'll ghost me. It was so awesome I'm wondering why I didn't go this route before. Paige would kill me if she knew I used her bed for sex. I'll wash everything before she gets back. She wouldn't be happy to know I was fooling around on the job either, but in my defense, it was after five o'clock. Technically, the end of the workday. I know, I know, it's a flimsy excuse.

"How's your dinner?" Max asks.

"Great. Everything I've tried here has been wonderful. I'm hoping we can get the chef's help at the inn for our breakfast menu. How's yours?"

He cuts a piece of steak. "Fantastic." His eyes twinkle, a smile playing over his lips.

I smile back, basking in the secret warmth of the *we just had sex and it was awesome* club. I take another bite of macadamia-crusted mahi-mahi. To think I was so stressed before. I don't even care that I still have work to do for my paying job tonight. Nothing can touch this afterglow.

"Earth to Brooke!" a woman exclaims.

I startle out of my dreamy state. My sister-in-law, Sydney,

is standing by our table, and I didn't even notice her approach. She owns the place. Her long auburn hair is up in a high ponytail, and she's wearing the black Horseman Inn T-shirt that all staff wear, with black pants and black ankle boots. "Hi."

I'm suddenly self-conscious about having dinner with Max. Sydney might bring it up back at her and Wyatt's house, where Paige and I stay when we're in town. Paige will ask questions, and I'm not great at hiding stuff. If Wyatt thinks there's any trouble in sisterland, he'll step in, playing the overprotective brother card, and "fix" the problem. I don't want him to fix Max. He's awesome just the way he is.

Oh, man, did I already fall for my casual, no-strings stress reliever?

Sydney smiles at Max. "Hey, Max." She looks between us curiously, a hint of a smirk on her face. I swear Wyatt is rubbing off on her. He's a big-time smirker. "How's your dinner?"

"Great," Max says.

I nod. "Really good."

Sydney socks Max on the shoulder and turns to me. "I grew up with Max, same grade. Audrey was crazy about him senior year of high school, until he dumped her for her own good."

Max rubs the back of his neck. "Ancient history. We're friends now."

"Just busting his chops," Sydney says to me. "Audrey's been pining for my big bro for *forever*, like real hero worship, with a few blips here and there for actual relationships."

Max shakes his head. "I'm sure she's outgrown that and sees him as a regular guy just like the rest of us."

Sydney looks thoughtful. "That's what I never got. In her eyes, he's some kind of warrior god—"

"A knight," Max says.

Sydney's jaw drops. "Did she say that? Like a knight in shining armor?"

Max shifts uneasily. "Don't tell her I said that."

"Max! Tell me. Did she say those exact words—knight in shining armor?"

He shrugs. "I always figured she turned him into a fantasy from one of those romantic adventure books she likes to read."

Oh, boy. Max is really spilling the beans on Audrey. Note to self: don't tell Max *any* secret fantasies.

Sydney slams her hands on her hips. "Romantic adventure books! How did I not know this?"

Max presses his lips together. "You didn't hear it from me."

Sydney shakes her head. "I just don't get her. If she secretly longs for adventure, why has she stayed in Summerdale working as a librarian? She's never even traveled anywhere. I need to talk to that girl. So secretive. You'd think she'd confide in me considering I've known her since *kindergarten*. Geez, now that I think about it, I'm pissed." She looks out the front window, her eyes narrowing. "I'm going to her place and demand she tell me everything right now."

Max holds up a palm. "She won't admit anything if you march over there demanding she talk."

Exactly. Max is surprisingly tuned in to sensitive issues. Or maybe he's just tuned in to Audrey. Is there still something there? My stomach drops at the thought.

Sydney sighs. "You're right. I just hate to see her stuck, you know?"

"She'll get unstuck when she's ready," Max says.

I push down my jealousy. Audrey must've trusted Max even more than her best girlfriend with everything she shared. That says something significant about him. He's trustworthy. And kinda wonderful.

Sydney nudges my shoulder, a knowing look in her eyes. "To think I was all set to match you up with Eli, and now he's married, and here you are with Max. He's one of the good ones, and I like that he's local. We gotta get you to stay here permanently."

"We're not together," Max says.

My gaze collides with his, oddly disappointed, even

though I was about to say the same thing. I don't want any of this getting back to Paige or Wyatt. "Just friends. We work together."

"Uh-huh," Sydney says. "Looking pretty cozy over here at a corner table for two."

The waitress, Ellen, a woman in her sixties with dyed blond hair, stops by to see if we need anything.

Sydney turns to her. "Would you say this setup here looks like two friends having dinner or a date? Objectively speaking."

Ellen winks. "Looks like two friends who might be leaning toward a date. Who's paying?"

"I am," I say immediately, even though I'm strapped for cash at the moment.

"We're splitting it," Max says, which is a relief.

Ellen cocks her head at Sydney. "Sounds like friends with potential to me."

They laugh and walk away.

I stare at my dinner, fighting the blush I can feel creeping up my cheeks. Didn't I say every emotion plays out on my face?

Max leans across the table. "They're bored at work. Don't listen to them."

I lift my head. "I just don't want it getting back to Paige." I leave Wyatt out of it. It's embarrassing to have an overprotective brother at my age.

His jaw clenches, and he leans back in his seat. "Right."

"I won't let her fire you or anything."

"I hope not." He leans close to whisper fiercely, "You went for me first."

I scowl. "Well, it wasn't like I attacked you. You reciprocated immediately."

He looks out the window into the dark of night. "It can't happen again."

Stung, I reply in a cool tone, "It never happened in the first place."

We finish dinner in silence. I'm so bummed I don't even

get dessert, even though I love the flourless chocolate cake here.

Ellen sets the check in the middle of the table. "Have a good night!"

"Thanks, you too," I say, reaching for my purse. I pull out my wallet.

Max snatches the check. "I invited you. I'll pay."

I open my mouth to argue and then shut it again. He's being kind, and I'm not going to end this night on a sour note. I had a fantastic time with him right up until I started complicating it by thinking we might continue this *whatever it is* together. One hookup, okay, two, means nothing. It was just stress relief. No messy emotions. I wish that were as easy for me as it seems to be for guys.

My gut does a slow roll. I thought Max was different.

"Thank you for dinner." I tuck my wallet back in my purse and pull out his check. "Oh, I almost forgot. Here's the next installment." I slide the check across the table to him.

He stares at it like it's a snake.

"The halfway mark," I prompt him. "Like I said before, you do great work."

He slowly lifts his head, his blue eyes reflecting hurt. I thought he'd be happy to get paid. He's been talking about accelerating the schedule. I assumed that was because he needed the paycheck and wanted to move on to his next project.

"What's wrong?"

He tucks the check in his wallet. "Nothing. Thanks."

"Max, c'mon, what's wrong?"

He shakes his head. "Nothing. This helps more than you know."

"Are you in debt?"

He meets my eyes, the warmth in them gone. "I'd like to avoid selling my house. My deadline with my brother is fast approaching. I'll give him whatever's left of this after I pay crew and cover supplies."

"What deadline?"

He explains about Liam's struggling farm, his pregnant

girlfriend, and the fact that technically Max, Liam, and Skylar are equal owners of the lakehouse.

"I love the house," he says. "Mostly nostalgic." He presses his lips into a flat line. "I should just move on. Liam did."

My heart aches in sympathy. I had no idea he needed money for family. And I've seen his lakehouse. It's special, being in the family for generations and in such a beautiful spot too. "What does Skylar think?"

He manages a half smile. "Skylar believes the universe unfolds like it should, though she hopes I can hang onto it."

"Now I bet you really wish you didn't underbid." I slap a hand over my mouth. "Sorry. I shouldn't have said that."

He stands abruptly. "Live and learn."

I stand too, sensing the evening going irrevocably south. He gestures for me to go out ahead of him. I walk to the front door, trying to figure out what I can possibly say to save the night. Everything started so lovely.

Max follows behind me like a dark cloud.

He walks me to my car. "Goodnight." He leans down, and for a wild moment I think he's about to kiss me and maybe everything is okay after all. Instead he kisses my cheek. "Thanks for the check."

"You earned it."

His lips twist to the side. Then he turns and walks away.

Wait, did that sound like he earned it for sex?

"I meant with all your good landscaping work!" I yell across the parking lot.

He lifts a hand in acknowledgment and climbs into the cab of his pickup truck. I rub my temple. Now why do I feel like I said the wrong thing again?

I drop my head with a sigh. *Because you did the wrong thing. Twice. You had sex with him, and then you paid him.*

10

I sit uneasily at the long light wood dining room table at Wyatt's house for what's become a tradition—Sunday family dinner. We're in the formal dining room, which is right off the kitchen, with a fireplace and a large red Persian rug over hardwood floors. The dining table seats twelve. Tonight it's Wyatt, Sydney, me, Paige, Kayla, and Kayla's fiancé, Adam. Wyatt sees his house as headquarters for the Winters-Robinson family. He hosts any and all special occasions from holiday dinners to weddings. Eli Robinson married Jenna here last New Year's Eve in the family room, and Sydney and Wyatt married outside earlier that year.

Wyatt and Sydney sit at the head and foot of the table, arguing playfully over which is the head and which is the foot, implying that only one is the real leader of the clan. It's a funny dynamic because they both insist on taking the end and, at such a long table, the other guests have to choose a side for conversation. Paige and I are next to Wyatt. Adam and Kayla are down at the other end of the table next to Sydney. We switch it up each week. Wyatt always invites us three sisters, while Sydney seems content not to invite all of her brothers. Only Adam because he's engaged to Kayla. I secretly think it's because Sydney thinks her brothers would get in the way of her leadership rivalry with Wyatt, stepping in to defend her, when she finds it immensely entertaining to battle him herself.

Normally, I'd be enjoying myself, but all I can think about is how I screwed up with Max. I should've paid him much earlier in the day so it was in no way connected to my later seduction. I don't know what came over me seducing him like that. We had dinner plans, which could've been a nice casual thing. Instead I threw myself at him.

And the thing is, I can't stop thinking about how awesome it was and how much I want to do it again. It's more than that, though. I really like him. I like that he keeps a sense of humor even when times are tough, like having to sell his beloved home for his brother's sake. Or getting knocked on his ass in a pond by my overzealous dog. He just petted him, called him a dope, and went back to work. I love that he puts his family first, helping his older brother out and his adoring younger sister. I love that he's so easy to talk to, so laid-back, and sweet too. A hard worker. Crap.

I'm in love with him.

I take a drink of water with a shaky hand. How could I let this happen? I was supposed to be careful, take it slow, keep things light. Major fail. And now everything's screwed up between us before we even had a chance. I should've called him, but I couldn't figure out the right thing to say. And now I know why. Because saying it was just stress relief is a lie. And I'm not sure the truth will be welcome news.

I'm driving back to New Jersey after this for my paying job and won't get to see Max until Thursday. Hopefully, by the time I get back, things will have cooled off regarding the check-after-sex incident. I'll explain—no, wait. I should drive over to his place right after this and be completely open and honest about how much I care about him. But what if he doesn't feel the same way?

Paige kicks me under the table.

"Ow!"

Her eyes bore into mine. "I was just telling Wyatt the inn is right on schedule and going according to plan."

"Brooke, I'm happy to contribute if things are tight," Wyatt says. "I want the inn to succeed."

It's so tempting to let Wyatt help. He's wealthy after several successful tech start-ups that he sold off, but Paige has been adamant that we can't accept his help. He'll take over.

I send Paige a beseeching look. *Just a little help?* Every single day I'm stressed over the budget and expensive delays. I had to give up the high-end antique bedroom furniture I wanted for the guest rooms. Now we're going with a simple rustic look with iron bedframes and machine-quilted coverings. No handmade quilts. The rugs were switched out to a simple fake sisal as well. And I had to scrap entirely Skylar's brilliant idea to lower the floors for a more spacious feeling on the lower level. At least Paige agreed to bring Skylar on board.

Paige gives me a subtle head shake.

I turn to Wyatt, his expression hopeful. He wants to help us so badly. I know he still feels like he's responsible for us as the man of the family. "We're doing great, but thanks so much for the offer."

He shoots a look at Paige, who looks pleased as she goes back to eating. "You're afraid I'll take over."

"I'm not *afraid* you'll take over," Paige says. "I *know* you'll take over."

"Only in a helpful way," he says, sounding offended. "Right, Syd? I know my shit, and I help businesses succeed."

"That you do," his wife replies easily. "But it's better when you're asked to help. Brooke and Paige have everything under control."

Wyatt turns to me, his brows drawn together over light brown eyes. "Be honest. I've seen you wound tight every time you come home. If you're stressed over—"

"We're fine," Paige says.

Oh, I'm stressed! My whole life is a blazing hot mess!

"Thanks for the offer." I give his arm a squeeze. "If we're ever seriously in need, you're the first person we'd go to."

He glances at my hand on his arm and picks up my hand. "Where's Paige's engagement ring?"

I tuck my hand in my lap. I can't lie to him, so I say nothing.

He pins me with a hard look. "Did you have to sell it to cover costs at the inn?" Wyatt doesn't miss a thing.

"I wanted to sell it," Paige says. "Who needs the reminder?"

Kayla pipes up from the other end of the table, her voice carrying. "No ring? Brooke, does that mean you're ready to date again?"

My head whips toward the other end of the table, though not to Kayla. I lock eyes with Sydney, begging her not to mention my dinner with Max. I don't want Paige to think I'm fooling around on the job, even though I now realize Max means much more to me than a fun time. It's bad enough I went into this business venture with big sister having the upper hand—more invested financially, more time on-site, cutting back her hours at work to just the weekends. She's always checking in to be sure I'm on top of stuff.

Sydney takes a drink of wine, looking serene. Good, she's keeping her mouth shut.

The room is quiet, all eyes on me.

"Well?" Kayla prompts. "Are you finally getting back out there? What's it been, six months?"

Leave it to Kayla to keep an accurate count. She's got Dad's head for numbers. And I broke that dry spell with the best sex of my life. And he said the same! That's incredible, right? It was incredible from start to finish because we're so in synch. I hope that means I'm not alone in feeling this way.

"Six months since what?" Wyatt asks.

"I'm guessing sex based on her flushed cheeks," Sydney answers.

"Nothing's going on!" I exclaim. "Paige wanted to sell the ring, and it was hers to sell. That's all that means." I take a long drink of water, feeling Wyatt studying me. I try not to squirm.

I decide to get ahead of any further questioning. I turn to Kayla. "Though, now that you mention it, I'm glad to stop pretending I'm engaged. It's much easier not to have to fabricate a whole complicated fake-fiancé story. I'd like to think if a cute guy came along, I could be as casual as every guy has ever been with me." *Right. You fell in love with him.*

Welp, the important thing is that I've successfully held off any further speculation from my family. No one would ever guess I had sex and then paid him. Or that I'm wishing I knew where things stood between us. I take a bite of mashed potato just to ensure I won't blurt anything else out.

I can feel people staring.

I chew and swallow. "What?"

"That doesn't sound like you," Wyatt says.

Paige narrows her eyes at me, like she knows I'm hiding something.

"Wyatt's right," Kayla says. "You're just not a casual person. You give one hundred ten percent to everything you do."

"True," Paige says. "That's why you're stretched too thin between your job and the inn."

I sit straighter, my shoulders drawing back with pride. Paige *does* believe I'm committed to our project. It feels good to have her respect.

My siblings study me. I avoid their eyes and go back to my dinner.

In the rare silence at the table, Adam speaks up for the first time. My future brother-in-law is Wyatt's age, thirties, a reserved dark-haired guy with a perpetually scruffy jaw. "Wyatt, we set a date for my bachelor party, the weekend before the wedding. You in?"

Wyatt rubs his hands together. "Yeah, I'm in. What's it gonna be? Drew's running it, right? I bet it's wild."

Adam cracks a rare smile. "Yeah. It's gonna be awesome. A guys' fishing trip. The whole weekend camping in Acadia National Park up in Maine."

Kayla giggles. Wyatt's never been camping in his life. He lived in the city before he moved here and before that Silicon Valley in California. We never went camping as kids either.

Wyatt shoots a significant look at Sydney, practically begging for help. She just smiles. He turns to Adam. "Cool. Is there a hotel nearby? I could just pop in for the fun fishing part." Wyatt's never been fishing either.

Kayla squeezes Adam's shoulder. "I told you he couldn't handle all that nature."

"Course I can," Wyatt says. "It'll be great. With the right gear…" He turns to Paige, who's traveled a lot. "Didn't you go glamping once in Tanzania?"

"I did," she says. "The tents were like luxury hotel rooms with a full staff to help."

Wyatt points at her. "Let's do that. I'll hire staff and find out where to get a few of those tents."

Adam shakes his head. "I prefer to keep it to the basics."

Paige smiles sweetly at Wyatt. "I'm sure you can rough it for one weekend to be there for your new brother-in-law."

"All natural, babe," Sydney says with a smirk.

Wyatt narrows his eyes at Sydney before turning to Kayla. "What're the women doing for the bachelorette party?"

Kayla beams. "Spa day."

Wyatt presses his lips together. He'd probably prefer to brave a women's spa day than the great outdoors.

"Kayla went fishing with Adam and had a great time," I put in. "Didn't you say that, Kayla?"

"Sure did," she says proudly.

Adam chuckles but doesn't comment on it. I bet he did all the work and Kayla showed up with snacks.

Wyatt exhales sharply and then abruptly changes the subject. "My sisters are all moving forward. Kayla's soon to be married, Paige is over her ex-fiancé, and Brooke is open to casual dating. Now as long as there's no jerks in Paige's and Brooke's futures, I can relax."

"Are you seeing someone?" Paige asks me.

Why does she ask me that after Wyatt mentions jerks?

I wave airily. "I see people all the time."

Wyatt stares at me. "You never could pull off a lie."

"I'm not lying about anything!" I exclaim. "Geez, can we go back to wedding talk, please?"

Wyatt leans forward. "Say the word. If there's a problem with a guy, I'll deal—"

"Did you hear that whimper?" Sydney asks loudly. "It sounded like Snowball might be stuck somewhere. Did someone shut a bedroom door upstairs?"

Wyatt bolts from the room, ready to rescue the little white shih tzu he adores.

I send Sydney a grateful look. My eye catches on Paige's curious stare. I force a smile and go back to eating. No one needs to know what happened with Max.

Or how scared I am that I'm alone in this.

Max

I threw myself into work this week, pulling double shifts to accelerate the schedule at the inn and finish up at the Bell estate too. I worked all weekend solo at the Bell estate. It's now Thursday, and my muscles are protesting what I've put them through. I can't slow down. It's mid-April, and the weekly mowing and spring cleaning of our regular clients has to be seen to as well. I wish I could afford more crew. I need to finish up at the inn so I can get the hell away from Brooke. Everything about what we did was a mistake. Hooking up at the inn. Having dinner together that felt dangerously close to a date. Getting my paycheck afterward. Male prostitute comes to mind.

It was a mistake. I'm going to collect my final payment and go.

I turn the waterfall on by the koi pond, and it flows in a rush. I crouch behind the waterfall feature and adjust the knob for a slower flow. I sit for a moment on a stone bench as a light breeze wafts by, pleased with the outdoor feature. All we need is the koi fish. I'm going to wait until all of the plantings for shade are in place to keep the pond from overheating. With the tall plantings around the pond and benches, it'll be like a meditation area. We put in a stone surround by the pond too.

My mind drifts to the next item on my agenda. The vegetable garden is planted. I still need to plant a floral section and then put in the stakes to fence the whole thing in. The dog play area is on hold, waiting on approval by the town planning board after the public hearing, so that could lessen my paycheck. It'll be tight without it, but I'm hoping whatever I can give Liam will help. I had another offer on my house, this time above asking price from a wealthy couple in Brooklyn. I asked for a week to think it over, saying I wasn't sure if I was ready to move. They then offered an even higher number.

I should just sell. That would be the logical thing to do, but my heart won't let me. I'm tied to the place and all its memories. I want it to stay in the family. Maybe Skylar will get married down the line and have kids who love to go there. That future is erased if I give it up.

I stand and stretch. Better get started on the flowers for the garden. I step out of the peaceful oasis, head toward the garden, and stop short. Why're there piles of dirt?

Shit! Scout got into the garden, and he's digging up all the vegetables. His long tail wags from behind a tomato vine staked in the ground.

"Scout, no!" I run toward him, waving my arms wildly. He runs in a zigzag through the garden, knocking into plants, and then zipping straight for me.

I back up. "Stop! Sit!"

He leaps up on me, his dirty paws slamming into my chest as he tries to lick my face. I push him down. No leash or collar. Where's Brooke?

I exhale sharply and go to inspect the damage as Scout follows me. He's dug up what looks like three-quarters of the garden. Dirt piles are everywhere, tiny leaves scattered, roots exposed, baby carrots half chewed, tomato stakes tilting wildly. This is going to cost me. Not that I'm paying for the damage. That's Brooke's fault for letting her dog off leash. This is going to cost me in time, which I can't afford. All the extra work I did is ruined. I need that final paycheck for completing this project. Now I have to start the garden over again.

I crouch down to replant some onions, and Scout jumps

on my back, trying to hump me. I stand and glare at him. "You had a field day, didn't you?"

He runs between my legs and circles me before doing a play bow. He's panting in what looks like a smile. Someone has to pay for this. "Where's your leash?"

I march back toward the house just as Brooke, Paige, and Spencer, the chef from The Horseman Inn, round the corner.

Brooke races toward us. "Scout! How did you get out here?"

"Your dog dug up the whole vegetable garden!" I shout.

She goes to grab Scout, and he dodges her. "His collar broke loose from the leash. I had him tied to the leg of the kitchen island, and he was sleeping."

Scout runs to me, jumping on my leg. I push him back and order him to sit. Finally, he does. I hold him in place with a hand on the scruff of his neck.

Brooke gives me an apologetic look. "This is terrible. I'd say he wanted to see you, but it seems he wanted to dig more."

I focus on Scout because now that I'm up close with Brooke again, memories I've been working hard to forget are flashing through my mind. Her long hair cascading around me in a silky curtain as she rocks against me, her face in ecstasy. I need to hang onto my mad to keep some distance between us. "Why did you bring him in the first place?"

She's wearing a peach filmy skirt, her legs bare in heeled sandals. My mouth goes dry.

"I only bring him when I'm here for a brief visit. Today I just stopped by to meet up with Spencer." She looks over at the ruined garden. "This is going to set us back. I'll get new stuff. Whatever you think can't be salvaged."

Scout wriggles under my grip, and I scoop him up in my arms. He licks my neck.

Brooke looks from him to me. "He adores you."

"I gathered that," I say dryly. "Can you get his collar and leash so we can get this menace under control?"

"Yes, let's go back to the kitchen."

"Guess we'll be going back there too," Paige says,

appearing by Brooke's side. "Nothing much for Spencer to see out here."

"Just as well," Spencer says. He's in his twenties, short brown hair, trimmed beard, and a bit of swagger in his step that says he's cocky about his skills. "Now you can start off with the items most useful to me."

Paige tilts her head. "And here I thought we hired a consultant chef to work with what we have."

"I'll send you a list," he replies smartly.

Brooke and I turn back toward the house, Paige and Spencer trailing behind.

Spencer continues, "Like I said, I don't have time to work here mornings, but I could train whoever you find to make the food."

"Just me," Paige says. "I'm the innkeeper, breakfast maker, and dishwasher."

"Any experience in the kitchen?" he asks.

"I do takeout and a mean buttered toast."

Spencer catches up to Brooke. "Please tell me you can do better than buttered toast."

"I can scramble eggs, but I'm only here part-time. I'm sure Paige and I can learn. How hard could it be?"

Spencer stops short, looking between Paige and Brooke. "So you're saying I get to train two beautiful women under me?"

"You're fired," Paige says flatly.

"Paige!" Brooke exclaims.

Paige jabs a finger at Spencer. "Under him? No, we're on top. We're *your* boss. We pay you."

My gut tightens at the reminder of my own pay situation. *Sex. Paycheck.* Scout barks in my arms. I continue resolutely toward the house.

Brooke and Paige are behind me, arguing over whether or not they're keeping Spencer. Right in front of him. Brooke declares they need him, and Paige says *anyone* can make breakfast. I glance over my shoulder. Spencer looks like he's enjoying the fight over him. Weirdo.

I walk faster, eager to put Scout back on leash and get back to work. I have to clean up the garden for the new plantings. "You've caused a lot of trouble," I tell him.

He gazes up at me, his big brown eyes shining with doggy adoration. It's hard to stay mad.

The downstairs of the house is relatively quiet when we get inside. Seems the crew has moved upstairs to work on the bedrooms and bathrooms. I take Scout to the kitchen and set him down on the floor by the island next to his collar and leash. I order him to sit, keeping one hand on his ruff.

Brooke rushes in a moment later. She grabs some paper towels and cleans his paws while I get his collar on him. I breathe in Brooke's floral scent that haunts my dreams. She's on her knees just like me. Scout's busy sniffing my hand. "I'm really sorry, Max. He's just not used to all this interesting stuff. Scout lived a sheltered life with me before at my apartment. I rented a small basement apartment in a house with a yard for him. Then he was at my mom's house and now at Wyatt's place, but Wyatt keeps the dogs on a short leash."

"As he should."

Her eyes are intent on mine, her voice soft with longing. "I think Scout knows you're a good guy. He really likes you. A lot."

My pulse kicks harder, and my voice comes out gravelly. "Thank Scout for me."

A crackling moment of tension hangs in the air, our gazes locked. I'm drawn in all over again.

Scout licks my face, jolting me back to reality. I push him away. "No more big wet ones."

Brooke stands and heads to the sink to wash her hands. I clip Scout's leash on him and stand, hanging onto it until Brooke's ready to take him.

Paige comes storming in. "We're not hiring him. Spencer Wolf can go to hell for all I care."

It seems Spencer left.

"But Sydney says he's a truly gifted chef," Brooke says. "That's an important part of the bed-and-breakfast experience."

Paige's eyes narrow. "He's completely inappropriate."

"So he's a little flirty," Brooke says.

"Brooke! He's the kind of guy who'd want a group thing!" She gestures between the two of them. "The three of us, and I'm sure it wouldn't be the first time!"

I bite back a laugh at Brooke's gasp of horror.

"No!" Brooke exclaims. "He did *not* say that."

Paige purses her lips. "Two beautiful women under me? How do you not hear it?" She slashes a hand through the air. "He's out."

"No, he can't be out. We both get a say in this."

"I'm burning his business card," Paige says grimly.

"Be reasonable," Brooke says.

Paige glances at me. "Did you hear what I heard? Cocky player who'll be impossible to work with?"

"Have you tried his food?" I ask. "The menu got a major upgrade when he got on board at The Horseman Inn. All fresh, healthy, farm-to-table food. And it actually tastes good too."

Paige grabs Scout's leash from me. "I'm taking Scout for a walk." She strides out the front door.

Brooke sinks against the island. "We need him. I can't believe she just unilaterally decided that."

"You're co-owners, so if you want him, then that means it's not over."

Brooke sighs. "I just came up with the perfect argument after she left. Isn't that always the way? When Kayla used to waitress at The Horseman Inn, she spoke fondly of Spencer. She said he flirted with everyone, and it didn't mean anything."

I force a straight face. "You want me to talk to him about appropriate boundaries in a professional situation?"

~

Brooke

I want to laugh. Max talking about boundaries after what we did together? But somehow all I can think about is how much I want to hug him, kiss him all over his handsome face, and then rip his clothes off.

He gives me a lopsided grin. "I could just lay it out. Spencer Wolf—very telling name for a three-way kind of guy, by the way—listen up. Always be respectful, keep your distance, never—"

I cut him off with a kiss. He yanks me against him, his mouth hungry on mine. The world narrows down to intense need. I've never felt anything like this pull.

I grab him by the front of his T-shirt and pull him backward with me toward the empty walk-in pantry. It has a door. Privacy. I bump against it and break the kiss just long enough to open it.

He follows, kissing me as we stumble inside and slam the door behind us. I'm suddenly starving for contact. I rapidly undo his jeans. He takes over, freeing himself, and then lifting me. I wrap my arms around his neck as he shifts us, hiking up my skirt, and then pinning me against the door. *More, more.*

He yanks my panties to the side and slides home, taking me to the hilt. *Yessss.* My breath stutters out, filled by him, aching and also so relieved to have him back.

White-hot pleasure fires through me with every hard thrust, his big hands gripping my hips, the momentum of his movements lifting me. Over and over and over. Need coils tighter and tighter, my breath coming harder. He angles me back just enough to slip his hand between us, stroking me. I buck wildly. His fingers are wicked, his thrusts deep.

Endless pleasure.

Fire. I'm on fire.

So close.

My body jerks, and then I cry out as the orgasm rips through me. His mouth covers mine, covering my soft moans as he pumps for his own release, bringing shockwaves of pleasure. He slams into me one last time, groaning into my neck.

Fuck. I seduced him again, and I didn't tell him how I feel. Though I wasn't alone in this seduction. He gave me a flirty reminder.

He kisses along the side of my neck, like he can't get enough of me. I let him, my head tilting back against the door to give him more access. I'm still throbbing.

He lifts his head, meeting my eyes. "This can never happen again."

"Invite me to your place tonight."

"We are *professionals*."

I stroke his beard. "I like it too much to stop."

He holds my jaw with one hand. "You more than like it. You love it."

We smile at each other.

"Come to my place tonight," he says.

"I can't. I'm working."

He lifts me off him and swats my ass. "You'll be there, and you'll like it."

"We'll see."

He grins, his eyes warm on mine.

I can't resist kissing him again, smiling as I pull back to look at him, hoping he can read the truth in my eyes. *I'm in love with you.*

"Max?"

"Yeah?"

"Brooke! Where are you?" Paige calls.

"Never mind," I whisper, quickly dressing and slipping out to the kitchen. Back to work.

11

At the end of the workday the next day, I relax with Max in the kitchen of the inn, having a drink and talking. I brought my favorite sauvignon blanc and coaxed him to try it. I'm sitting on the island, and he's leaning against it next to me.

He looks over at me. "Still stressed?"

I smile and nudge his shoulder with mine. "You definitely helped with stress relief." We hooked up last night at his place, plus earlier that day in the pantry. Last night I apologized for the timing of his check after our first hookup, and he was okay with it. I'm not sure how much of his forgiveness was driven by lust and the fact that we were alone at his place, but hey. Everything's cool again between us.

"It's the kind of thing you need a daily dose of for maximum effect." He cradles my jaw and pulls me in for a kiss. "Doctor's orders."

I smile against his lips. "Which doctor is that?"

"Dr. Love."

I pull away, laughing even as my pulse jumps. "Seems appropriate."

He takes another sip of wine. "This stuff grows on you." He stills. "Wait, what's appropriate?"

I lift one shoulder. "Dr. Love. For me, it's not so casual anymore."

He cups the back of my neck, pressing his forehead against mine. "You're crazy about me."

My heart jackrabbits against my rib cage. "Yes," I say softly. "How about you?"

He sets his glass down and pushes my legs apart, standing between them. "I thought we were keeping this professional, Ms. Winters."

"Max," I say unsteadily as his big hands stroke the outside of my jean-clad legs. His hands land on my hips, pulling me closer until I'm fully pressed against him. Desire spikes instantly.

He takes the wineglass from my hand and sets it next to his. My pulse accelerates.

His fingers tunnel into my hair, his lips hovering over mine. "I'm crazy about you too."

I wrap my arms around his neck, happiness bubbling up inside me. His lips graze mine before fitting more firmly against me. He shifts, kissing along my jaw, his beard rubbing against me deliciously. His teeth scrape my neck before he sucks on the cord of my neck. My head drops back as his hands slowly stroke up my inner thighs. Need coils tight within me, an insistent throbbing, begging for his touch.

The front door creaks open, and we break apart. Max steps away, and I see my sister Paige, her eyes wide, taking in the scene. My heart thunders. She left for the city a couple of hours ago. I know this looks bad. The two of us in the kitchen with a bottle of wine, me sitting on the island, Max next to me.

"Just having an after-work drink," I say brightly. "It's been a long week. How come you're not in the city?"

Paige approaches, studying me from my lips to my cheeks, which are probably both pink, and to my hair, which is probably mussed from Max's fingers. "My Saturday morning appointment cancelled. I went to Wyatt's, and he wouldn't stop bugging me about the inn's financials, so I thought I'd stay in my apartment here for a little peace and quiet." She gestures between me and Max. "Are you two…"

"Chilling with some wine," I say. "Yup."

She steps closer, inspecting my neck. I cover it with my hand instinctively. Beard burn, a love bite, I don't know what's there, but I have a feeling Max left some evidence. "Brooke! What the hell? Is this how you spend your time when I leave? Fooling around with our contractors?"

"Not all of them!" I exclaim.

Max stiffens. "Brooke has been nothing but professional. And I take this job seriously. It was just an after-hours drink."

Paige isn't buying it. "How long have you been seeing each other?"

"We're not seeing each other," I say. "Except at work. And, okay, I visited his lakehouse and went on a boat ride. Happy?"

Paige scoffs. "A boat ride. Right. Here I am busting my ass around the clock while you're using our brand-new kitchen as your personal playground."

"Don't be mad at her," Max says. "I take full responsibility."

"Max, no," I say. "I seduced him. He just went along with it."

Paige throws her hands in the air. "Are you not all in, Brooke? Tell me now. As it is, I poured my life savings into this venture, which was *double* what you contributed, and I cut my hours back significantly to dedicate to this project. You're here two days a week, and in that time you seduce one of our contractors! Are you concerned at all about making this inn a success? We're going to lose our shirts, *I'm* going to lose my shirt, if it fails."

I look to Max. "You should probably go. Paige and I need to have a serious talk, and I don't want you in the middle."

"You sure?" he asks.

I nod, touched that he'd want to stay to show his support. "I'll call you later."

He gives me a sympathetic look, nods at Paige, and walks out.

Paige crosses her arms. "Well? Did I get into this with a dud partner?"

"Okay, I may not have had as much money to put in, but

I've also put in my entire savings. I gave up my apartment to save money and moved in with Mom, which is not easy, because she always wants to know if I'm eating enough, sleeping enough, and finding time to exercise, which I'm not!"

Paige hitches a thumb toward the front door. "One could argue that he's exercise." She shakes her head, looking like a know-it-all big sister. "Never get involved with someone you work with, especially when you're signing his paycheck. Really, Brooke, it's so unprofessional of you."

"I can't explain it, he just…" I sigh. "Look, I'm as committed as you are to the inn. I couldn't give up my paycheck from my job, but I managed to work out a remote situation, which bleeds into the weekend, because I can't do it all. I'm stretched very thin, stressed all the time, and Max is like a calm oasis in all of that chaos."

Paige takes a deep breath. "Is it serious?"

"I don't know." *I hope so.*

Her voice softens. "So end it. He's a distraction, and you've got enough on your plate. I need your full focus on the inn in the short amount of time I have you here."

My gut turns over, leaving a sick feeling. I don't want to end it with Max. I feel good when I'm with him, and it's not just the sex. I love his easy humor, his warmth, the way he really cares about his family and his work. He's that rare good guy I never seem to find. How can I let him go?

I can't. I care too much about him to do that. I don't dare say the L word out loud, but I feel it deep in my heart. I need to wait for the timing to be right.

Paige's voice is sympathetic. "You went and fell for him, didn't you? You always get in deep, and then you get hurt."

"I'm fine. I won't get hurt." I take a deep breath. "I'm not ready to cut him loose yet."

She gives me a skeptical look. "How can I count on you to pull your weight here when you're pulled in so many directions?"

I bristle, aware once again I have to prove myself to my big sister. I'm not willing to give up Max, but there is something that would bring me some relief. "I'll ask my boss if I can cut back to part-time. It'll take the pressure off, and I can focus more here. I'll propose two days a week in the office only, and then I'll leave my work there. The rest of my focus will be one hundred percent here."

"Can you afford that?"

"It's not ideal, but, worst-case scenario, I can always crash with Wyatt." Worst-case scenario meaning if the inn fails. I try never to say those words out loud, afraid to jinx our business venture.

She grimaces. Living with Wyatt wouldn't be her first choice. She loves her independence.

I let out a breath. "And we're getting close to the end here. Seven more weeks. I wanted to find new consulting work locally while I help part-time here, so I'd be quitting eventually. It's the right time for shifting to part-time."

"Is Max going to be a problem? What if things go sour and then you still have to see him here working, expecting a paycheck." She shakes her head. "Never fool around with someone you hired."

I hold up a palm. "Okay, I get it, but it's a little late for the big-sister advice." I can't find the words to explain what Max does to me, how good I feel when I'm with him. He's not just the guy working on our landscaping. He's so much more. "I'll keep it strictly after hours. Like tonight."

She exhales sharply. "I don't even want to know what else went on here when I wasn't around."

My mind flashes to the pantry and that first time on the air mattress in her apartment. "You really don't."

I settle in at my desk in the open office space at work on Monday morning, my nerves on edge. I sent an email to my boss, Bill, over the weekend about setting up a meeting today. He agreed, and it's almost time. I've prepared a speech about how I would like to keep working here; scaling back to one client could make part-time work a possibility for me. I'll lose my healthcare and benefits, but hopefully it'll work out in the long run. Paige and I will try to get some benefits going through the inn once we're operational.

I'm so nervous I'm sweating through my yellow floral blouse. I paired it with black trousers and block heels. My usual business-casual work outfit. Everything will be fine. I'm a valuable employee. I've been working here for four years and always have great performance reviews. Unfortunately, that hasn't translated to more responsibility as lead architect. I'm always in a supporting role here, which is why I was so psyched about taking the lead on the inn and future projects I hope to have for homes.

It's time.

I make my way to his large glass-enclosed office and step inside, smile firmly in place. "Morning, Bill." He's a tall bald guy in his sixties, who dresses impeccably. Today he's wearing a gray blazer, crisp white shirt, and gray trousers. All of it custom made to suit his frame.

He stands and gestures toward the door. "Shut the door behind you."

My heart leaps to my throat. Not a good sign. I shut the door and take one of the burnt orange cushioned chairs in front of his mahogany desk. "Thanks for meeting with me. I had a proposal for you regarding my work hours."

He holds up a palm. "Brooke, we're letting you go."

My heart pounds. "What! Why?"

"Look, this is never easy. We need to make some cuts and, frankly, you've had one foot out the door for a while now. The remote days weren't working for me. Your work has been spotty ever since last January when you bought the inn. Truth is, we can't afford to keep someone on who's not pulling their weight."

I can barely catch my breath, my mind racing along with my heart. I grip the arms of the chair, trying to steady myself. I lick my dry lips. "Okay, uh, what about part-time? I could work on one dedicated client in a support position."

"You'll receive four weeks' severance pay. Please see HR on your way out."

My mouth gapes, my gut in a cold knot.

Bill shuffles some papers on his desk, dismissing me.

My eyes get hot. *Don't cry, don't cry.* "Am I the only one being let go?"

"Three more after you," he says. "Good luck with your inn."

"Thanks," I mumble, making my way to the door on shaky legs. I can't believe this. No safety net. Poof! Gone. Now it's just the inn.

I walk back to my desk in a daze. I've never been fired in my life. I guess technically I was laid off since it wasn't just me. He said they had to make some cuts. I was an easy choice since he wasn't happy with my remote work. *Shit.*

I move through the rest of the morning in a numb state of shock. I clean out my desk, sign a few forms, turn in my key card, and then go to Mom's house.

Scout's thrilled to see me the moment I get back unexpectedly mid-morning. I hug him around the neck, and he licks the tears from my face. Mom's at work at the university. I let out a shaky breath and go to the kitchen, grabbing the notepad she keeps by the phone. I scribble a quick note telling her I'm moving to Wyatt's house for the foreseeable future. I'll give her all the details tonight. I'm not ready to rehash the morning's events. Her sympathetic tone will have me in tears. No time for tears. I've got work to do.

"We're going to be full-time at Wyatt's," I tell Scout. "Would you like to play with Snowball and Rexie?"

He runs in a circle and barks.

"Okay, let me pack our stuff, and we'll get going. Time to make our dog-friendly inn a reality. You can test out all the doggie features. Dog play area, dog guests, all within a dog-friendly town."

He cocks his head like he's confused.

I sniffle and wipe my tears. "You'll see."

≈

After I get Scout settled at Wyatt's house with his dog cousins, I show up at the inn, surprising Paige, where she's in an upstairs guest room, holding paint swatches up to the wall.

"What're you doing here?" she asks. "Did you pull back to part-time already?"

"I pulled back to no time." My voice cracks. "I was laid off."

"Oh no! Brooke! I'm so sorry. Was it because you asked to cut back your hours?"

"Nope. He had to let some people go, and he wasn't happy with my remote work. He said I've had one foot out the door ever since I bought the inn. See? I am committed to our business."

She hugs me. "I'm sorry I doubted you." She pulls back. "It's been a lot of pressure for both of us. We're almost there. I got started on a simple website this morning, and Sydney said she'd help us with our marketing plan. One of the things she mentioned was announcing our opening at the ground breaking for the new animal shelter next month. You know, get some word-of-mouth going with all those animal lovers."

I smile. "That sounds great. The Inn on Lovers' Lane. Do you think we should come up with a more dog-friendly name?"

"I just bought the domain name for the Inn on Lovers' Lane. Ah, what the hell. We can always buy another one if we come up with a better name. It's only money, right?"

I give her arm a squeeze. "We'll keep what we've got. I'll go check in with Gage. I saw him in the master suite's bathroom on my way to see you."

"Skylar's stopping by around five to go over color schemes for the bedroom suites with me. Well, I guess with us now. You should join us."

"Absolutely." I pull my phone from my purse and add it to my calendar.

I find Gage hauling a tub with iron-clawed feet into the master bath with three other guys. I'll wait to check in with him.

I head downstairs and take a moment to check my email. I click on an email from the Summerdale planning board. My stomach lurches. *Denied.* They denied our request to build a dog play area! The whole inn revolves around the dog concept!

I rush to the stairs. "Paige!"

She appears at the top of them. "I just got the same email. The neighbors must've put up a fight." She rushes downstairs. "What're we going to do? This was our whole theme."

"I know. It was what made us stand out from the competition. We even added a patio for more space for the dogs and owners." My voice cracks. "I ordered dog water bowls and some doggy signs with cute sayings to put up around the inn. It was going to be heaven for Scout."

"Shit."

My gut churns. The whole dog concept was inspired by Scout and how dog friendly Summerdale is. They even have an annual dog swim in Lake Summerdale. My plan is falling apart. Was I ever fit to be lead architect? Maybe Bill saw what I couldn't. I'm not ready for this kind of responsibility. I should've thought of clearance with the planning board early on, but I didn't because I underestimated how big a deal a dog play area would be to the neighbors. My shoulders droop. What a crap day.

"We still have the breakfast part," Paige offers.

I exhale sharply. "Every B&B has that. What do we have that a zillion other B&Bs in the area don't have?"

Paige mumbles something I don't catch. She's at just as much of a loss as I am.

"I'd better go tell Max," I say, already on my way out. He'll have to cut the dog play area out of his plans, which means he could be finished here even faster than the two weeks he anticipated.

His truck isn't here. I walk around to the backyard. He's not there either. Strange. It's not like he finished the job here. There's still a good amount of landscaping, plantings, and trees to add to our property. He didn't even leave a crew member behind. I tense, my teeth grinding together. Dammit!

I pull out my phone and call him. The moment he answers, I snap, "Where are you?"

"I'm short a guy on crew and had to get started on another project before we lost it. I'll be back at the inn on Thursday." Today's Monday. Unacceptable.

"So we're not a priority for you now that you're nearly finished?"

"Of course you are, but I'm juggling a lot of priorities. Don't worry, I'm coming back."

"We lost the dog play area, so guess what? You can wrap up here even faster than you originally thought."

"Shit. That was a sizable..."

"Can you return the fencing and artificial turf?"

"I sure as hell hope so."

"Max, you need to get back here right away and finish what you started."

"I told you Thursday."

"If you're not here by tomorrow morning, you're out."

"What!"

"I need contractors I can depend on."

"Brooke, what's going on? You sound really wound up."

I press my lips tightly together, my eyes hot.

"Are you okay?"

Everything comes out in a rush. "I lost my job, lost the entire concept for the inn, and now I'd like to accelerate opening the inn, seeing as how I've got no regular paycheck, but I can't do that when the property is half planted and missing all the stuff we were promised."

"Did Gage finish the renovation?"

"I'm talking to him next." I don't know how much faster Gage can work. "Honestly all I can think about is the fact that you're supposed to be here and you're not. I need you to do what you said you'd do. That's called professional integrity."

"I'm sorry to hear about your job. I really am. And I know you're upset, but don't take it out on me. The work will get done on time as promised."

I huff. "If I can't count on you, then forget it. Okay? Just forget it."

"Fine. I'll be there tomorrow morning."

"Thank you."

"I'll be finished by the end of the week and collecting my final payment." He hangs up with a quick bye.

I pace the yard. Somehow that doesn't make me feel any better. He'll be done and gone. I'm not even sure he'll want to keep seeing me after I just pulled rank as a pissed-off client. Suckiest day ever.

12

Max

I screwed up big time. I accelerated the timeline on the inn, finishing on Thursday, mostly so I could get my final paycheck, and then zipped back to the wealthy homeowner's property I started on a few towns away, where he promptly fired me. He was angry we excavated for the new patio and landscaping beds and left him hanging for three days. Dammit. The word-of-mouth business could've paid off huge in that town. And I still haven't gotten my final paycheck from Brooke. She said they were having cash-flow problems and couldn't pay me until Friday.

I park in the street in front of the inn. It's now Friday, I lost a lucrative client, and I want my money. Not just want, I need it. Besides, I did everything we talked about. I step out of the truck and inspect the front yard. The plantings aren't looking so good. Evening frost looks like it got the best of them. I'll have to replace them out-of-pocket next month. May is always better for new plantings. I know that, but with the pressure from Brooke and my brother, Liam, breathing down my neck, I acted irresponsibly. He gave me until the end of the month, which is tomorrow. He can't pay his mortgage next month if I don't sell our house. I thought I had it all worked out, and it's just falling apart.

Damn Bellamy genes. I fell back on my true nature, irresponsible just like Dad. First, I was irresponsible with work and then with Brooke. Things have been tense between Brooke and Paige all because of me. I knew it was unprofessional to hook up with her, but I couldn't seem to help myself. Okay, I know why. She's irresistible. And, if I'm honest, she means a lot to me. I haven't felt like this about a woman in a very long time.

Still, I'm mad at her. She pressured me into getting back here, and that's what screwed up stuff with my new client. Maybe some distance between us is a good thing. It's not like I'm going to marry her. I'm not cut out for marriage. I should end it before either of us gets in too deep.

I stand there for a moment, stewing in everything that's gone wrong in my life. Everything I did has been in a valiant attempt to save my family home. It's time to face facts. Liam's going to lose his farm if I don't sell. He's going to be a dad soon, and I want my niece or nephew to have a home. So it's time to sell mine. It was stupid to hang onto it for as long as I did. I got an offer significantly above asking, I counteroffered with an even higher number, thinking they'd drop out, but they agreed. I pull my phone out and make the call to Pete, my eager real estate broker.

The moment he answers, I force the words out in as calm a voice as I can muster. "It's Max Bellamy. Go ahead and accept the offer on my house."

"Yes! You're doing the right thing, Max. It's not often you get an above-market offer like this. It's gold. I'll call their rep right now. We'll have it all squared away by Monday."

"Okay, thanks. Bye."

I press the heels of my hands against my eyes, my throat clogged with emotion. Would Mom be upset that I sold out? She's not around to ask anymore. I'm the only one mourning the loss of the place.

I drop my hands and text Liam the news, including the surprisingly high sale price. He calls right away. "Great news! Aw, Max, this couldn't have come at a better time. We just found out we're having twins. I was panicking about it, all that responsibility, not to mention the bills, and then you came through!"

My chest tightens. I hope he's not going to take after our dad and bail. I walk down the street to talk in a quiet spot. "You sound like Dad talking about the bills and responsibility."

"That's because I'm going to be a dad. If you take it seriously, bills and responsibility are a heavy burden. I'm sure it'll be worth it."

I relax because he sounds so happy. "Congrats on twins. That's big news."

He laughs. "We just keep cracking up about it because it's such an overwhelming shock. I'm sure once they get here, we'll be better prepared. The doctor says its identical twins, which is even wilder. We'll need to color-code their clothes in the beginning. Two of everything. It's nuts in the best possible way."

I smile. "Real happy for you."

"Thanks, bro. And thanks again for coming through for my growing family."

"Of course. That's what family's for."

I hang up and walk over to the inn's front door. I did the right thing selling. Doesn't make it any easier.

I let myself in the unlocked front door and look around for Brooke. Construction is still going strong upstairs and downstairs. It's payday. The check will be less with the absence of the dog play area, but it's still much needed. I have to cover paycheck for crew, and I'll give whatever's left over to Liam. I'm not sure how long it'll take for the sale of my house to go through.

I find Brooke and Paige in the kitchen, huddled over a laptop, whispering fiercely.

"Hey," I say, striding over to them.

Paige promptly shuts the laptop and straightens. "Half the plantings up front are dead."

"Early frost last night, I know. I'll replace them next month, no charge. It was probably too soon for young plantings."

"We'll pay you once work is completed," Paige says.

"Paige, I told you we can trust him to come back," Brooke says.

Paige glares at her. "Your judgment is suspect since you two are a thing."

I clear my throat. "I live and work in town. This is my biggest project to date, and I would never do anything to jeopardize it or my reputation."

"Except sleep with your client," Paige says under her breath.

"I'm writing the check," Brooke says, meeting my eyes directly, her tone cool and professional. "I took out the dog play area supplies and related labor. Were you able to return that stuff?"

"Yeah, minus ten percent."

Brooke turns to Paige. "He shouldn't be out that ten percent. It wasn't his fault. We'll cover that, and he said he'll cover the dead plantings. We're good here."

Paige shakes her head. "The plantings were his responsibility anyway. Final payment when final work is complete. That's how any professional contract works. You can give him partial payment today."

They start arguing in fierce whispers, turning their back from me and walking away.

Look what I did, causing more tension between the sisters. I never should've gotten involved with Brooke. Paige wouldn't be digging her heels in so much if she didn't think Brooke was favoring me unfairly.

"This isn't how I do business!" Paige exclaims. "Fine! We'll see how this plays out. Just don't say I didn't warn you." She strides out of the room, her jaw set tight.

Brooke gives me a small smile. "Sorry about that. I'll pay you your final check. I know you're good for it, and I'm the one who rushed you to finish the job." She pulls out a checkbook from her purse, double-checks the number on her laptop, and writes it out.

I shift uneasily. Irresponsible. It's my biggest flaw, and look what happened. I lost a big client, disappointed another.

The sisters are fighting because of me. I wanted to leave here with glowing referrals. Now Paige doesn't respect me and thinks I'm not professional. Brooke is being kind, but I know what I have to do. It's time to step out of the picture.

She hands me the check, and I tuck it in my back pocket. "Thanks."

"Sorry about earlier. Paige and I have been butting heads lately. There's a lot of pressure with the inn. She just lost a major sale at her other job, so cash flow is tight all around. Not your fault."

"I don't want to add to any pressure you two are under." I pause, lowering my voice. "She's right, you know. It was unprofessional of me to cross the line."

Her chin lifts. "I crossed it too. I crossed it *first* as a matter of fact."

"But I went along with it when I knew it was wrong." I look over her shoulder, avoiding her eyes. "I think it's best if we don't see each other anymore."

"Because of Paige, or is it me?" Her voice sounds small.

My gut clenches. "Look, I'm just not a commitment type of guy. Trust me, it'll be easier now than down the line."

"Oh." She blinks rapidly, opens her mouth, and shuts it again. "If that's how you feel."

I take a step back, needing to keep my distance. "Take care, Brooke. Good luck with the inn."

Her green eyes reflect hurt as she searches my expression.

I look away, my gut churning. I never wanted to hurt her, but it's for the best.

"Bye, Max," she says softly.

I walk out, free of all responsibility. No more house, no major job, no woman. Just me and my regular mowing and lawn maintenance jobs. Status quo. I should feel free, exhilarated even; instead I'm weighed down more than ever.

∼

Brooke

Two weeks of nonstop work at the inn has taken a toll on

me, but I can see the light at the end of this tunnel. It's the first weekend in May, and it looks like we can open the inn in June. Losing my job was a blessing. I needed the time here, and it took the burden off Paige's shoulders. I should be ecstatic. But every moment I'm not working, I'm thinking about Max. I miss him so much. Paige was right. I always get in deep, and then I'm the one who gets hurt. I don't know why I keep letting down my defenses. It's like I can't seem to help opening my heart even when I know better.

This time was different, though. I didn't just feel warmly toward Max. I fell in love. He was different than most guys I meet. I felt safe with him and at the same time excited. I didn't even know passion like that existed in real life. He was always so genuine and straightforward, a refreshing change of pace. Even breaking up with me, he was honest. He could've just walked off with his paycheck and never called again.

I still don't get what went wrong. It nags at me, this unsettled feeling that we aren't done.

I pace my bedroom at Wyatt's house. It's Saturday night, and I should be relaxing, but it's impossible. My mind keeps turning over what happened with Max. This is exactly why I wore Paige's engagement ring for so long. I needed time to regroup after so many bad experiences, and then what do I do? I fall for the first guy to smile at me.

I rub my temple. He has a great smile, warm and full of good humor. He was the bright spot in my day. And the whole time I was getting in deeper and deeper, he was still operating under the assumption that we were just having fun together. I thought when he said he was crazy about me, like I was with him, that meant something deeper. Maybe he was just saying it back to me without really meaning it. We *were* about to hook up again.

I could show up at his open house tonight and spill my guts. Tell him I'm in love with him, and I don't want it to end. Kayla told me Max sold his house, and the sale is final as of next week. He's having one last blowout party to say goodbye to it. It's an open house, which means anyone in town can just show up. I know how much that house means to him. He must be so sad to let it go. My chest aches in sympathy. So many of his family memories are tied up in the only house he's ever lived in. Some of them with family who've passed away.

I need to go over there in support of Max as a friend. I walk over to the mirror above the dresser and touch up my makeup. I can do this. He ended it, and I have to accept that. I should just take him at his word that he's not a commitment type of guy. I'd like a committed relationship, so clearly there's no future.

I suck in air, working hard not to cry. I'm not going to cause a big emotional scene or try to win him back. If he's upset about his house, I'll just say something comforting. No way I'm going to make a fool of myself and blurt everything I'm feeling. But, if the mood seems right, I'll say I hope we can stay in touch. No pressure.

I brighten, feeling good about my plan. I get to keep my dignity, and maybe we can still see each other as friends. I don't have to say bye forever. He's still friends with his ex Audrey, after all. This is something people do. Well, I've never done it before, but it *can* be done. I go downstairs and take the dogs out for a pee break and then lock up behind me. Just me here. Wyatt and Sydney are at The Horseman Inn, working tonight, and Paige is in the city for her weekend gig.

I drive over to his house, memories of my time there flashing through my mind. Sitting on his deck talking, out on the boat, in his bed. Nope. Dial it back to friend town. He's hurting over the loss of his house. *Lower expectations.* I'll get closure. That's all.

When I arrive, there's a few people I don't know sitting out on the deck, drinking and talking. I head inside and spot Kayla, Audrey, and Jenna sitting on the living room sofa. I join them, sitting on the arm of the sofa next to my sister. Jenna is a tall blonde, owner of Summerdale Sweets, the bakery in town. Audrey smiles at me, her blue eyes kind. To think I was once jealous of her relationship with Max. Now we share an ex. My chest aches. *Don't think about it.*

Kayla pops up from the sofa to give me a quick hug. "Glad you came out tonight. Drinks are in the kitchen. Max is manning the grill out back."

"Thanks." She knows something happened with Max because Paige has been snippy about the fact that we were involved at all. Wyatt overheard, of course, since this all went down at his house. He's been surprisingly quiet on the subject. I bet Sydney made him swear not to interfere. She's been a calming influence on him. Thank God because he has a long history of butting into my life (and my sisters' lives) in the name of big-brother responsibility.

"How's everyone doing?" I ask.

"Good," Audrey says.

"How's the inn?" Jenna asks.

I smile. "Coming along nicely. We're looking to open in June. Still need to come up with a new hook. The dog play area was cancelled, and we're rethinking the whole concept."

"What's the name of it?" Jenna asks.

"The Inn at Lovers' Lane," I say. "Because it's on the end of Lovers' Lane."

Her brows lift. "There's your concept. Honeymooners."

"I'm not sure if Summerdale is enough of a destination spot for that."

"It could be," Audrey says. "We're like an oasis for city people. Lots of fresh air and nature."

Kayla grabs my arm. "Weddings! Remember Jenna had her small wedding at Wyatt's house? It was like an elopement but with close family and friends. You could specialize in elopements! So romantic!"

My brows knit, thinking that over. "Isn't there a waiting time for the wedding license?"

"Only a twenty-four-hour waiting period," Jenna says. "We just went through this. And couples can get it anywhere in the state, and it's good for sixty days. All you need is an officiant. You could ask Levi the mayor, or one of you could get an online officiant license and act as witness."

Kayla claps. "I love weddings. It's big business, Brooke. Elopements at a romantic inn would be so unique. You could have them just for the wedding couple or for their inner circle."

"Inner-circle elopements," I echo. "I like that."

She nods enthusiastically. "It wouldn't have to be complicated either. Flowers, chocolate, champagne, done."

I smile. "That actually sounds amazing. I have to run it by Paige, but I love that idea."

"I can help you guys get set up," Kayla says. "That way I can be part of the inn too."

I put an arm around her and give her a squeeze. She's a biostatistician, so we didn't include her in the inn, thinking she wouldn't have much interest. She must've felt left out of our sisterly venture. "I'd love that. And you're the expert on wedding planning after helping plan Sydney and Wyatt's wedding and now your own."

"One day I'll help you and Paige plan your weddings," she says.

I take my arm off her. "Yeah, don't hold your breath."

"Just because things didn't work out this time doesn't mean they never will," Kayla says. "Don't give up hope, okay?"

I stand. "Yeah, sure. I'm going to get a drink."

"Who were you seeing?" Jenna asks me.

Kayla answers for me. "Max."

I glance at Audrey, who used to date Max.

"He's a good guy," she says. "What went wrong?"

I shrug. "It's complicated. I'm hoping to get a few things straight tonight."

"He ended it, didn't he?" Audrey asks.

"How did you know?"

"Besides your brave face?" she asks with a gentle smile. "He's always the one to end it for one noble reason or another. He has serious commitment issues. I heard he ended his five-year relationship because she wanted to get married, and he didn't want to lead her on, knowing he would never marry her."

Max had a five-year relationship? That doesn't sound like

someone with commitment issues. "So he's against marriage?"

"Seems that way," Audrey says with a shrug. "But who knows? Maybe he's matured. He's twenty-nine and could see the world differently than when he was younger. Don't give up hope."

She doesn't sound too reassuring. And that's the second person to tell me not to give up hope in the last five minutes. Do I look as sad as I feel?

"Thanks," I say flatly. I'm not sure if that show of support was more demoralizing or encouraging.

I make my way to the kitchen for a drink and find Max standing there, talking to Skylar and another petite brunette with a sympathetic look on her face. There's a platter of freshly cooked burgers and hot dogs on the kitchen table that no one's paying attention to.

Has Max already moved on to someone new?

She's pretty—long dark hair, amber eyes. Wait, isn't that Queen Snowflake from the Winterfest ball? She looks different without the crown and formal wear. Today she's wearing a faded black T-shirt with ripped jeans.

Skylar opens the pantry door and takes a picture of the height lines where she and her brothers were measured growing up. "Take one with me now," she says to Max, standing with her back against the measuring spot.

Max pulls his phone out and snaps a picture. Then the other woman directs them both in place and takes their picture.

"Thanks, Sloane," Skylar says. She hugs Max. "I'm going to take some pictures of my room. I want to preserve my mural."

"Sure," he says softly.

She walks toward me on her way out and gives my arm a squeeze. "It's tough to say bye to this place. We just found out the new owner plans to demolish it and build a big two-story house on the spot."

"Oh, I'm so sorry."

She nods. "Thanks."

"I'll go announce the food's ready," Sloane says.

He puts a hand on top of her head just like he does with his sister. "Thanks. Could you get me a beer from the cooler on the deck when you're out there?"

"You got it." She glances over toward me. "Hi." She turns to Max. "Looks like someone wants to talk to you."

His eyes meet mine, registering surprise. "I didn't know you were coming."

Sloane gives me a small wave. "I'm Sloane. Max and I are best friends, no worries." She holds up her hand. "I'm engaged. To your brother-in-law, actually, Caleb Robinson."

She knows who I am. I brighten, pleased that Max talked about me with his best friend. "Then we're practically family. Congrats on your engagement." I almost blurt we might do weddings at the inn, but I don't want to get drawn into a long conversation. I need to talk to Max alone.

She gestures to the platter of food. "Want something before I take it to the masses?"

"No, thanks."

She nods once and carries the platter to the door by the deck. "Little help here!"

Max rushes over and opens the door for her. He walks back into the kitchen and leans against the counter. "Guess you heard I sold the place."

"Yeah, I know it's hard on you to let it go. I just wanted to stop by and see if you were okay. It really is a nice place. Do you know where you'll be moving?"

"Temporarily living with Rob Murray." He gestures toward the deck. "Sloane's dad. He's the owner of Murray's, the repair shop in town. He gave me my first job, and he's been like a dad to me. After that, I guess I'll try to find something I can afford in town or close by. My business is still mostly here. Trying to branch out."

"How's that going?"

He runs a hand through his hair. "Back to mowing and maintenance. Growth will be slower than I'd like, but what can you do, right?"

"Right." My heart squeezes. He's going through something, but it has nothing to do with me. I keep my feelings to myself, not wanting to burden him. "I just wanted to see if you were okay." I take a step back. "I'll let you get back to your party." I turn and walk away, my throat tight.

I stop in the living room to tell Kayla, Audrey, and Jenna bye.

"You just got here!" Kayla exclaims.

"I saw Max," I whisper. "We talked. He's mourning losing his family home. I think he'll be cheered up more by his friends and sister."

Kayla gives my hand a sympathetic squeeze. "You can hang with us. Adam's working in his workshop tonight. He doesn't like big parties."

It's just her and Audrey now. Jenna's with her husband, Eli, on the other side of the room.

Just then, a man with longish dark hair and a scruffy jaw approaches with a red Solo cup. Oh, it's Sydney's oldest brother, Drew. He owns the dojo in town. There's a quiet intensity to him. Coiled power barely held in check.

Drew hands the cup to Audrey. "Here. It's pinot grigio."

Audrey's brows shoot up. "Drew! I didn't see you come in."

He rubs the back of his neck. "Just got here."

"Stealth," she says. "How'd you know my favorite drink?"

"You order it at the bar all the time. You operate like clock-work, exactly the same every time."

Her lips form a flat line. "Thanks. I do branch out on special occasions."

Kayla pipes up. "Did you bring this with you? I didn't see any pinot grigio in the kitchen."

The tips of his ears turn red. "It was in there," he mutters. And then in a polite tone, he looks to me and then Kayla. "Can I get you two anything?"

Kayla holds up her cup. "Working on my chardonnay, but thanks."

"I was just on my way out."

He shoves his hands in his jeans' pockets. He's not drinking, not talking. Just standing there, his eyes locked on Audrey.

Her cheeks flush, and she takes a sip of her drink. "Very good. Tastes just like the kind I buy for home."

He relaxes a fraction. I wonder if he asked Sydney what kind to get and bought it himself.

"Read any good books lately?" she asks him.

I give her a little wave. She smiles at me. Kayla pulls a sad face. *Sorry.* Not sticking around when Max doesn't seem to want me the way I want him. He ended it, and I have to accept that and move on.

I head for the door and rush down the stairs. I'm halfway to my car when I hear my name.

"Brooke, wait!"

I freeze and slowly turn, my heart pounding.

Max jogs down the stairs and walks right up to me. Close. His voice is gravelly. "Stay."

13

Max

"I was thrown seeing you again," I say, struggling for the right words. "It's been a helluva couple of weeks."

Brooke searches my expression. "Okay."

I take her hand and guide her toward the lakeshore. "Wait here. I'll be right back with a blanket for us to sit on."

She nods once.

I dash back to the walk-out basement and grab a large green beach blanket. I race back to the beach, half afraid she left. I wasn't as warm to her as I should've been. I missed her so much it was like a never-ending ache. I hadn't realized how much that was part of my sadness over the last two weeks until I saw her again. I thought it was all about losing the house. Maybe I was using that as an excuse so I wouldn't have to face the loss of the best thing to ever happen to me. I'm not ready to say goodbye.

I lay out the blanket and gesture for her to take a seat. She does, sitting with her legs crisscrossed.

I sit next to her. "I'm glad you stopped by tonight."

"We've missed you around the inn," she says softly.

"Has Paige been missing me all that much? I got the feeling she thought my work was subpar and I was unprofessional."

She turns to me, her green eyes intent. "I missed you. And I don't want you to feel any pressure to reciprocate or anything like that. I hope we can be friends."

"Friends," I echo, taken aback.

"Your best friend is a woman. You're still friendly with Audrey. Seems like that's something you do."

"I don't feel the same way about them as I do with you."

She presses her lips together, her eyes soft. "How do you feel about me?"

"Not like a sister or a friend! I, uh…" I search for the words. "It's like this. I did the opposite of what I wanted to do by selling the house. That was the responsible thing to do, right? And I thought it was also being responsible to end things with you, which is also the opposite of what I wanted to do, and I'd at least like to take that one back."

"Because I'm stress relief?"

I lean close. "The best stress relief of my life."

She stares out at the lake for a long moment. "Right. Here's the thing. I feel like I misunderstood the situation between us, and I get it now. You said commitment isn't your style." She hesitates, her brows drawing together. "At least not with me. I'd better go." She stands.

I stand too. "That's it?"

She shrugs. "I'm not sure there's anything else to say. I have a terrible history of choosing men who are wrong for me. I always get hurt. I'm hurt right now, and I'm—" Her voice chokes. "I'm so damn tired of it."

"I never meant to hurt you."

She presses her lips tightly together and looks away.

Audrey called me Mr. Wrong before, as opposed to Mr. Right. Maybe I am. I seem to screw up every relationship. Maybe I do that because I know in the long run I could never handle the responsibility of a commitment.

Then why does my gut feel like a lead weight at the thought of another goodbye?

Is it me that's the problem here or her baggage?

"What would change your mind?" I ask, trying not to

sound desperate. She did say she has a terrible history with men. I hate to think I'm part of that in her mind.

She gives me a sad smile and squeezes my arm before turning to go.

I stare after her, racking my brain for how to fix this. "What do you want?" I yell after her.

She turns. "Not this."

My gut does a slow churn. Can't get much clearer than that. I'm not what she wants.

She walks away.

I sink to the blanket and stare blankly out at the water that's been a constant companion to me my entire life. No more roots. I'm free, completely free of all ties, answering only to myself.

I'm so lost.

∼

Brooke

A week later, Paige and I attend the ribbon-cutting ceremony for the Summerdale Animal Shelter. There's a good crowd here. We've brought our new glossy brochures to announce the opening of our inn. At long last, the end is in sight. The renovation is complete. We're adding the finishing touches to the interior, and we're opening in two weeks in time for Memorial Day weekend. We're already fully booked that weekend with just one customer. Harper Ellis, the famous actress who was raised here, booked the entire place. She's bringing along her husband, Garrett Rourke, her bodyguard, a nanny who helps with her daughter, Caroline, and another couple—actress Josie Abbott and her husband, Sean Rourke. Garrett and Sean are brothers and part of the royal Rourke family, though they were raised in Brooklyn. Harper's grandmother will stay in the first-floor suite, even though she's local, because she wants to spend every waking moment with her great-granddaughter Caroline. If the fame of those two actresses doesn't bring some buzz to the inn, the royal connection certainly will. All in all, we couldn't ask for a better grand opening.

The Inn at Lovers' Lane is going with a romantic bent, thanks to Kayla. Instead of being the only dog-friendly B&B around, we're going to be the destination for elopements. If anyone's looking for an intimate romantic getaway, we can be that too. Hopefully, couples will come back to celebrate their anniversary with us. Full confession—Kayla is the master-mind behind all the romance stuff. Paige and I have little experience to draw from, and we don't have the fanciful imagination our little sister does.

Kayla even went the extra mile and arranged for us to meet with her wedding planner in Clover Park, Hailey Camp-bell, who was happy to advise us and even offered to send people our way if she hears they'd prefer an elopement. Mayor Levi has agreed to be our officiant when needed. We're also advertising online and in bridal magazines. Now if we could only book an elopement, we'd be set. Ironic that Paige and I, who have no serious relationship and are a long way from a wedding of our own, are now in charge of bringing wedded bliss to others.

I miss Max, but I tell myself it's for the best. He wanted casual and, I quote, "the best stress relief of my life." I can't blame him for not being where I'm at, but I want more for myself, a relationship with a future.

A microphone rings out feedback as it turns on, bringing me back to the moment. Dr. Dominic Russo, the veterinarian who spearheaded this effort, stands with the mike in front of a large red ribbon. He's in his thirties, short dark brown hair and kind brown eyes, dressed nicely in a blue button-down shirt and navy trousers. He's holding a Boston terrier, who rests his front paws over his shoulder. The dog looks old and rather haughty, like he's above all this commotion.

Next to Dr. Russo are Summerdale's first King Frost and Queen Snowflake—Caleb Robinson and Sloane Murray—wearing their crowns and sashes. They're a cute couple. Caleb is known for being a male model with some major campaigns. Wyatt recently showed me Sloane's car repair show on the

Turbo channel. I had no idea since I never watch that channel. It debuted a couple of weeks ago. Wyatt's so into it, he says he wants to learn how to repair classic cars. I think he just wants an excuse to buy cars. I'm nothing but supportive, though, because it's always better when Wyatt has a focus other than his sisters.

"Thanks for coming out today in support of Summerdale's first animal shelter. I'm Dr. Russo, your local veterinarian, and this is PJ, everyone. Short for Pretty Jaded." He turns so we can all see the Boston terrier's haughty expression.

The crowd laughs.

Dr. Russo hands the microphone to Caleb, who smiles, saying, "I can personally vouch for the amazing animals available for adoption. Dr. Russo takes good care of them and has a network of volunteers who walk them and help them get socialized. I adopted my Siberian husky, Huckleberry, from him and couldn't be happier."

Sloane pulls the mike down toward her. "Please ignore his ridiculous name. He's quite brilliant and way more dignified than the name implies."

Everyone laughs.

Caleb takes the mike back. "He's a goofball. I would've brought him today, but he gets too excited with a crowd and tries to show off. Unlike PJ here, he's Mr. Mellow." He hands the mike to Dr. Russo.

Dr. Russo smiles. "True. PJ's twelve and available for adoption, so if you want a dog who'll nap in your lap all day, he's your guy. PJ and I want to thank you all for coming out today. The support I've found here in Summerdale for the shelter and all the animals in need has been overwhelming. If you'd like to see the plans for the shelter, they're in the lobby of my office out front. I'll just give you the highlights—a room just for the cats with kennels as well as open space for them to climb and play, and a large room for the dogs with an enclosed area in the back of the property for the dogs to play."

Paige and I exchange a look. There's the dog play area we tried to implement. Though this one is exclusively for shelter animals and there's no residential homes nearby. Dr. Russo's office is at the edge of town on Route 15, the major thoroughfare leading out of Summerdale.

He continues. "And there's going to be a reception room and a private room for prospective adopters to meet one-on-one with the animal of their choice. In fact, we have a couple of cats and a few dogs available for adoption today if you'd like to meet them in my office after this. Please say you do."

Mayor Levi Appleton, a handsome guy with a full beard, approaches, saying into the microphone, "I'll take a look at the dogs." He hands Dr. Russo a pair of scissors.

Dr. Russo isn't done his push for adoptions. "That's great. We've had several successful adoptions. The dogs we currently have all have good temperaments. Like this guy." Dr. Russo holds up PJ and then sets him down. PJ immediately looks up at him like he wants to be picked up again.

A woman with a camera stands nearby to record the event for the online newspaper, the *Summerdale Sheet*. I've taken a peek at the paper before; it's mostly local news, including a police blotter with the funniest crimes I've ever seen, many involving missing items that were later found and noises that turned out to be nothing. They sure keep the cops busy around here. Ha-ha.

Dr. Russo finally cuts the ribbon. Everyone cheers and claps. My sister-in-law, Sydney, and Spencer, the chef of The Horseman Inn, roll out a cart with a large rectangular sheet cake. It's decorated with a dog and cat face and says Congratulations! King Frost and Queen Snowflake pose with Dr. Russo next to the cake for pictures, and then Caleb starts slicing pieces while Sloane hands then out. Dr. Russo is flooded with well-wishers.

Spencer walks away with Sydney, giving me and Paige a salute as he walks by. Paige gives him a deadpan look. I just smile. We've been working with Spencer to come up with a breakfast menu that's enticing and also not too hard for me and Paige to make. Paige has been cool toward him, saying he's arrogant and a player. He has good reason to be, let's say, confident. His chef skills are amazing. And I've found him to be a good teacher. Patient and thorough, always praising our efforts. Paige insists his praise is suspect and he really just wants to get with one or both of us. Who can blame Paige for being jaded about players? Her ex-fiancé had a well-known womanizing reputation before she dated him. Everyone said he'd changed because of his love for her; even she believed it. Then he bailed on the wedding a week before, running off with a flight attendant he'd just met.

The crowd disperses, some chatting while they eat cake, some heading toward the vet office to check out the available animals for adoption. We left our brochures in the lobby next to the plans for the shelter. Hopefully a lot of people head that way. We didn't want to leave them out here in case the breeze blew them away.

I turn to Paige. "What do you think about a pet for the inn? Either a dog or a cat. It might make it more homey for the guests."

"Uh, no. What if someone's allergic?"

"We didn't worry about that when we had a dog theme."

"Yes, but that was because we were going to push that angle in our marketing, so only people who had dogs would be interested." She looks around. "You know, I'm glad we went the elopement route. It broadens the possibilities of who'd book the inn."

"Couples in love."

"And their closest family and friends. We use the elopement angle, but then we also say there's room for guests to share in the happy event. And we can have a nice reception for them on the patio or under a tent in the yard. Kayla's brilliant."

"We should've included her more."

Paige nods. "I assumed she wouldn't be into it. Busy with planning her own wedding and her career, but she has the soft touch we lack." She gets a text and checks it. "Speaking of, our sweet little sister just arrived. She wants us to meet her out front."

"That's mysterious. You think she adopted a dog?"

She grins. "Most dogs could run circles around Tank.

Could be funny." Tank is an English bulldog Kayla lives with ever since she moved in with her fiancé, Adam. The dog is so lazy that he'll only do half a walk, and then Kayla pulls him the rest of the way in a big red wagon with a shaded canopy and a fan. She totally spoils that dog.

Paige and I make our way through the crowd, stopping to chat a few times with people we know. Summerdale is feeling more and more like home to me. We've met a lot of people through Wyatt and Sydney.

In the front lot, Kayla waves to us from where she's standing with Max next to his Bellamy Landscapes pickup truck.

My heart thunders in my chest. Max's blue eyes are locked on mine with serious intent. He's holding a bouquet of roses.

Kayla wiggles her fingers at me and heads inside the vet's office.

"Give him a chance," Paige says under her breath. "He wanted to make a grand gesture. Kayla and I helped."

My head whips toward hers. "You helped? When did you have time?"

"Early this morning. I'll go stand by our brochures and push the inn. You deal with your Romeo over there." She walks away.

I'm at his side before I'm even aware of moving. "Hi."

He hands me the bouquet of roses. "For you."

I take them, breathing them in. This is only the second time I've ever gotten roses. The first time was after a dance recital when I was a kid. "Thank you."

"Come for a ride with me. I want to show you something."

I nod.

He opens the passenger door of his truck for me and shuts it behind me. There's a small gold box tied with ribbon from my favorite chocolate place in New Jersey.

He gets in the driver's side and hands me the gold box. "Kayla told me what you liked. I drove down yesterday to get them."

"Max, wow, I'm overwhelmed. I haven't heard from you in a week and…I guess I thought you were moving on."

He shakes his head. "Not possible." He starts the truck and pulls out of the lot. "I'm learning to let go of the past, and that's made me more open to the future."

Butterflies dance in my stomach. This sounds promising. "You mean your house?"

"The house and all the memories tied up in it. I closed on it this week, got the check, and paid out my brother and sister their share. It's a fresh start for me and long overdue."

I'm quiet, thinking about what a fresh start would mean for Max. He's lived in Summerdale his whole life; his business is here. Is he thinking of moving somewhere else? A new career? Something to do with us?

"I'm getting a fresh start too," I say. "My job is at the inn now, living here in Summerdale. I hope to pick up some architecture projects and buy a place of my own one day. There's actually a run-down cottage on the corner of Lovers' Lane that would be ideal, but I can't afford it right now."

"What would you do with it? Knock it down and start again with a larger house?"

"No way. It's so darling. It reminds me of an old English cottage with the shutters and window boxes. I'd renovate the inside, fix up the exterior; maybe down the road I'd add an addition to the back of it for more space. I noticed a separate outbuilding in the back. Apparently, it used to be an artist's studio. They went bankrupt and had to sell."

"You sure know a lot about it."

I look out the window, recognizing the route he's taking. We're heading toward Lovers' Lane. "Wyatt's the one who brought it to my attention and filled me in on the history. He knows I'm always curious about interesting houses."

"Cool." He hits the accelerator, racing past the old cottage as we head down the street.

I point out the window, craning my neck to see. "There it goes."

He slows down again, driving us to the inn. It must be. There's nothing else down this road except a few homes.

"Something going on at the inn?" I ask.

"You'll see."

He pulls into the driveway, parks, and steps out. I hop out, dying of curiosity.

I stop short on the front walk, my hand flying to my mouth. Not only did Max put in the plantings along the front walk and the front of the inn that he promised, but he also planted so many beautiful flowers. There's a rosebush, red and pink tulips, cheerful daisies, and more flowers I don't recognize, an explosion of color.

He appears by my side. "These are just the spring blooms." He points. "That plant will produce pink flowers in summer, and these over here will change with the seasons, spring, summer, fall." He gestures to more plantings.

"Max, you really came through. Has Paige seen all this? She should be here."

"Ah, yeah. Paige and Kayla helped me get it ready this morning." He takes my hand. "There's more." He guides me around to the back of the house. More plantings and flowers. And there's a wooden wedding pergola decorated with greenery and bunches of roses in pale pink and white.

He guides me under the pergola. "For your new elopement theme. I decorated it just so you could get an idea. If you want, I can grow some climbing vines along the side, and then you'd just add fresh flowers for the wedding." He gestures to the vegetable garden in the side yard. "I added some rosebushes and a few other flowers Kayla said are popular with brides."

My eyes well. "I can't believe you did all this. It's just so wonderful. Thank you."

He takes both my hands in his, gazing into my eyes. For a wild moment, it feels like we're the bride and groom under the wedding pergola. "Brooke, you're more than just stress relief for me."

I blink back tears. "Oh-kay."

He exhales sharply. "I have feelings for you. Deep feelings and this here is my way of saying…I love you."

My breath catches, my heart racing. I was so sure he didn't feel the same way I did.

He closes his eyes for a moment. "If I'm alone in this—"

I kiss him. "You're not alone in this."

He pulls back, gazing into my eyes. "I've felt so lost over the past couple of weeks, losing you, losing my house, and then it finally hit me—you're home for me."

I throw my arms around his neck. "That is the most romantic thing anyone has ever said to me. Me too, Max."

He kisses me and then folds me into his arms, holding me close. "Good thing we're home for each other since we're both currently homeless."

I laugh and lean back, stroking his beard. "I was so afraid I was alone in this, all these deep feelings, but now. I'm just so —" My voice cracks. "I'm so happy." My eyes well. "I love you too."

He cups my cheek and kisses me long and deep. "One more thing to show you. Follow me."

"There's more? But you already did so much."

"Well, when you finally realize that you're actually good at being responsible, you want to run with that."

I follow him to his truck. "Wait. You thought you were irresponsible? But you have your own business, you helped your brother, you adore your sister—"

"Yes, and it finally hit home that no matter how much I take after my irresponsible father, I'm not him. Liam was so grateful for my help he's naming one of his twins in my honor. Identical boy twins. He asked me to be godfather. You only do that with someone you really trust."

We get in the car. I grab the chocolate box and offer him one. He takes a candy, and I take one too. "Mmm, so good. Max, I could've told you that. It's so obvious you keep your commitments. You went above and beyond for the inn. I'm sure all your clients feel you're dependable."

"Yeah, but none of them named a kid after me." He starts the truck and backs out of the driveway. "And part of being godfather means he wants me to take care of his kids if anything happens to him and his girlfriend. God forbid, but that's what he said."

"Quite an honor."

The drive is short. He stops in front of the cottage and steps out. The first thing I notice is the For Sale sign now says Sold. The second thing I notice is the newly planted front landscaping beds with neat hedge bushes and wildflowers.

I turn to him, eyes wide. "Did you buy my cottage?"

He smiles and kisses me. "I bought a cottage that needs renovating. I'd love to be your first client. Check it out. Tell me how you'd fix it up."

I blink rapidly, eyes hot, throat tight. My first job on a cottage I loved on sight. Maybe one day I'll live here with Max.

He gets out of the truck and walks around to my side, opening my door and guiding me out. "Do you like the wildflowers? I thought they fit better with the cottage."

"I love them."

He walks with me to the front door and unlocks it. The inside is circa 1960s with hardwood floors and vintage lighting fixtures. The walls are painted a swirly yellow fresco. There's a pass-through window from the front living room to the kitchen, which has white-painted cabinets and stainless-steel appliances. My mind whirls with possibilities.

I peek down the hallway to check out three bedrooms and a full bath. I rush back to the living room. "Can I see the artist studio in back?"

"Sure can."

He lets us out the back door by the laundry room. I walk over to the small white-sided building with skylights and large windows.

Max stops in front of the door. "No pressure, okay? This is just an idea."

My brows draw together in confusion.

He opens the door and gestures for me to go inside. I step into a light airy space that shines from floor to ceiling like it was recently cleaned. There's a vintage tilt-top drafting table, as well as a desk with a cushioned chair by a window. I stare at it. "It looks like an office. Is this for your business?"

"It's for you."

I whirl, my jaw dropping.

His voice is gravelly. "All of this is for you."

"Just me?" I ask, my voice strained. It's the most magnificent gift I've ever received, but I want *him*.

"I'd like to make a home together." He frames my face with his large hands. "Would you consider marrying me?"

Hot tears leak out of my eyes. "Yes, I would consider that very seriously."

He kisses me. I throw my arms around his neck and return the kiss with wild abandon.

He hugs me, speaking near my ear. "How seriously?"

"I can't believe you bought me a house."

"I bought it for us. Hold on, let me do this right." He pulls a diamond ring from his pocket and goes down on one knee. "Brooke Winters, I love you, and I'm so damn grateful you came into my life. Will you do me the great honor of becoming my wife?"

"Yes!"

He slides the ring on my finger. I hug him, speechless and completely overwhelmed.

He pulls back to smile at me. "I've never been so happy."

"Me too!" I look around, ideas already cranking through my mind. There's a galley kitchen to my left and a doorway at the back of the studio space. "Is there a bedroom back there?"

"Sure is. Thinking of trying it out?"

I race back there to check it out, noting the dimensions, the small closet, and the en suite bathroom. "I'll definitely use this as my office, but the nice thing is we could also use it as a rental space if we wanted."

"I thought it'd be just for us for a while."

"I need to sketch this out as well as the cottage. Oh, Max, I have so many ideas already. I can't wait to get started on the renovation."

He rubs the back of his neck. "Maybe hold on that. I spent everything I had on the house."

"Got it." I mentally measure the window size in here and consider shifting the closet to make room for a larger bathroom.

"You're planning the whole thing in your mind, aren't you?"

"Yes," I say absently, pulling out my phone tape measure app. "Just need a few measurements."

"Guess it's all me for the wedding planning."

"I'll ask Kayla to handle it. She loves that stuff."

He grabs me and pins me against the wall. "You know what I love?"

"What?" I ask, breathless.

"You." He kisses me, and things get out of hand fast. Next thing I know, he's lifting my leg and positioning himself. "We have to make this place our own."

My breath comes harder. "Sex in every room. It's the only way."

"I love the way you think."

And then there are no more words. Only a drive to join— our bodies, hearts, and souls. *Bliss.*

When I come back to earth, Max dresses me and then scoops me up, carrying me through the studio space and out the door.

He grins. "Now I have to carry you through the threshold of the cottage. Kayla told me it's some kind of wedding tradi- tion. I had to make sure you agreed to be my bride first."

"We seem to be good at doing things out of order. First the house, then marriage."

"As long as we end up together, that's all that matters."

EPILOGUE

Max

It's the end of June, and I'm waiting in my tux under the wedding pergola for my bride. How cool is this? We're the first couple to elope at the inn. We did the inner-circle package, which means our friends and family are here. Brooke hired a primo photographer. Get this—our wedding pictures will be on the inn's marketing material, the website, and submitted to bridal magazines for potential articles. What a way to capture the moment.

Kayla married Adam the first week of June in an elaborate ceremony and reception at the Bell estate. Brooke and I decided then and there, we wanted a small intimate wedding. Don't get me wrong, Kayla's wedding was fun. It's just not our style. Kayla and Adam just returned from their honeymoon in Hawaii last weekend, looking tan and happy.

My brother Liam's my best man, and my best friend Sloane is my best woman. Brooke asked Kayla to be her matron of honor and Paige her maid of honor. She couldn't choose between her sisters, which is why I have only two on my side to match. My sister, Skylar, is doing a couple of readings for us. Brooke's mom, Cynthia, is in the front row, and of course I had to invite Sloane's dad, Rob. He's my honorary dad. Rob seemed to hit it off with Cynthia when they met last night. Interesting combo—a history professor and a mechanic.

Skylar waves to me from the end of the short aisle, holding an eager Scout by the collar. His golden retriever fur is looking fine after his visit to the groomer. He has a pillow strapped to his back with the rings. I've been working on getting Scout not to jump on me when he wants attention. Let's see how this goes.

I check in with our officiant, Mayor Levi, and then give Skylar a nod. She points to Wyatt to start the music, a slow processional.

I slap my thigh. "Scout, c'mere, boy."

Skylar releases him, and he trots down the aisle, head and tail high, mouth open in what looks like a smile. The small group of well-wishers *ooh* and *aah* over him.

"Good boy," I say. "Wait."

He stands patiently while I retrieve the rings from the pillow. Then I give him a vigorous pet, and he leans against my leg. I scoot back, not wanting to get golden retriever fur on my tux. Skylar calls him, and he races down the aisle toward her.

She orders him to sit, but he's got too much momentum and doggy excitement for that. He jumps up on her to lick her face. She laughs and pushes him back down and then snaps a leash on him, leading him to lie down at the end of the aisle.

Paige makes her way down the aisle in her peach brides-maid dress, holding a bouquet of white roses. My pulse picks up. It's really happening. For so long I thought I wasn't cut out for marriage. I thought I had the bad Bellamy genes, irresponsible and not able to handle a big commitment. But you know what? All it took was the right woman to make me see how awesome a life together could be.

Kayla walks down the aisle next, but my eyes are glued on the woman behind her. There she is—my beautiful bride. She takes my breath away. The white gown fits her snugly with a lace top and beaded straps. The bottom skirt seems to float around her in layers. Her hair is up with flowers woven through it. She's carrying an elaborate bouquet of pink and white roses.

I blink a few times to clear my vision, unexpectedly teary. I just love her so much. She told me I'd be a great dad since I'm so good with Scout and Skylar. Not that a dog and little sister are the same thing, but still. It means a lot to me. My whole life I thought I wouldn't have what it takes to be a dad with the bad example I had. Brooke believes in me one hundred percent.

She beams a smile at me that makes my eyes water. Finally, she reaches my side.

I cup her cheek. "So beautiful."

"I love you."

"I love you too."

Someone clears their throat. Oh. Guess we have some vows to get to. Mayor Levi Appleton signals to turn off the music, and we begin.

My life starts again at this moment with Brooke by my side.

Brooke

I'm trying not to be a weepy bride, but Max is making it difficult with his teary eyes. I sniffle and a tear escapes. I'm barely aware of the people around us, all of my focus on the man I love with all my heart.

I lose it when he says his vows with such deep-throated sincerity. He wipes my tears with his thumbs. I spot Sloane over his shoulder, wiping her eyes too.

I make it through my vows with a steady voice and only a few catches in my throat.

"I now pronounce you husband and wife," the mayor declares. "You may kiss the bride."

Max cradles my face in both hands and gives me a tender kiss. Then we hold hands and face our small gathering of friends and family, smiling.

They cheer and clap for us as we walk down the aisle. An

outdoor wedding at the inn was the perfect choice for us. It's where it all started, and there's nothing more appropriate for a landscaper than to enjoy nature during his wedding. And I got to include Scout!

At the end of the aisle, Max grabs me in a hug.

I hug him tight around the middle and look up at him. "You made me cry with your weepy eyes."

"No, you had weepy eyes first, and then I had slightly weepy eyes in sympathy for you."

I laugh. "Right."

He takes my hand and kisses the knuckles. "You overwhelm me. I can't believe how lucky I am."

"Me too!" I exclaim happily.

Kayla appears by my side. "Congratulations!" She hugs both of us at the same time. "Spencer wants to know if he should bring out the food for the cocktail hour." Spencer agreed to cater our wedding. I'm hoping we can regularly hire him to cater weddings for the inn. It would be a side gig for him. His main job is still head chef at The Horseman Inn. His boss, my sister-in-law, Sydney, was okay with him occasionally working for us. She figures it'll encourage our wedding guests to try out The Horseman Inn while they're in town. Too bad he's still on Paige's bad side.

"Absolutely," I say. "I'm starving. I was too nervous to eat earlier."

"What were you so nervous about?" Max asks. "Did you have doubts?"

"No, not at all. I just wanted everything to be perfect."

"That's why you have me," Kayla chirps. "I'll go let him know. In the meantime, have some champagne." She gestures toward the white tent in the yard. There's a small dance floor, as well as long tables for food and drink. Round tables with white tablecloths surround the dance floor. This was the setup that Wyatt and Sydney had at their outdoor wedding at their home, so we totally copied them. It was the most stress-free wedding planning ever. Mostly thanks to Kayla. She might've missed her calling as a biostatistician. She rocks at wedding planning.

Spencer walks outside wearing a black button-down shirt and black pants and holding a large platter, followed by two more servers dressed the same.

Max and I follow him to the tent. The food platters are set on a long table next to the champagne. I gesture for our family and friends to come closer and help themselves.

Paige scrutinizes the food. "What happened to the stuffed mushrooms?"

Spencer bristles. "I made an executive decision. The mushrooms weren't in good shape. Instead we have sweet potato slices topped with cheese and cranberries. I also added bacon-wrapped dates."

"You're supposed to run menu changes by your client," she says. "Pro tip."

He steps close enough that she has to lift her head to meet his gaze. "I make decisions based on the quality of food available to me the day of. I'm known for fresh farm-to-table food. *Pro tip*—it tastes better. Try the sweet potato slices."

Her eyes narrow.

"I'll try one," I say, taking a slice. Max does too.

"They're really good, Paige. Try one," I say.

Spencer picks up a slice and offers it to her. "Try it."

Her eyes flash. "Force-feeding a client. Nice."

"I'm offering it," he says through his teeth. "Do you see me forcing it down your big mouth?"

She gasps. "Big mouth!"

He shoves the slice in his own mouth and chews ferociously before turning and walking back toward the inn.

Paige plants her hands on her hips. "Can you believe that guy? We're never hiring him again."

"Look around," I say. "Everyone seems to be enjoying the food."

She glances around. "They're just hungry."

"And the dinner menu sounds spectacular," I say. "As good as any fancy restaurant in the city."

She takes a deep breath. "Sorry to be a crank. Something about him puts me on edge. Anyway, as long as you deal with him and not me, I guess it's okay."

"And I'm happy to do that, but don't forget we've got a full house here next weekend for the Fourth of July, and he's scheduled to handle the barbecue. I'll be on my honeymoon." Max and I are flying out tomorrow for our honeymoon in Bermuda.

She glances at Max and then hugs me. "Of course. Don't give it another thought." She heads for the champagne table and tosses back a healthy swallow.

"He seems fine to me," Max says.

I keep my voice low. "I think he reminds her of her ex-fiancé. Noah was really, let's say, confident bordering on arrogant. She thought it was a good quality at first and then later not so much."

Max kisses me. Soon we're surrounded by well-wishers asking us about the inn and our plans for our new cottage. That's the nice thing about a small wedding. We can have real conversations with everyone close to us.

Before I know it, Kayla announces dinner is on its way and asks everyone to find their table. She made cute name placards for everyone with a calligraphy pen. She thinks of everything.

Wyatt sticks around after everyone's left for their tables, holding me in place with a hand on my arm. I grab Max's hand to keep him with us.

Wyatt looks unusually serious. "I thought long and hard about what to get you two for a wedding present. And I thought the best gift would be a home tailored to your specs."

"We have a home," I say.

He hands me an envelope. "It's for your renovation budget. Go wild. Make it yours."

I don't even have to look inside the envelope to know big brother has given us an extremely generous gift. "Wyatt, it's too much."

"How do you know that?" Max asks, taking the envelope. He peeks inside and sucks in air.

Wyatt hugs me and whispers in my ear, "Nothing is too much for my little sister. Congratulations."

My eyes well. "Thank you." Wyatt has tried his best to be

a dad to me and my sisters ever since our dad died. He's only four years older than me, but that one event aged him into a maturity well beyond his years.

He kisses my temple and then shakes hands with Max.

"Thank you so much for your generous gift," Max says. "I can't wait to see what Brooke comes up with. She's brilliant."

Wyatt grins. "That she is. And thank you for getting her to move here permanently. Things were looking dicey there with her job in New Jersey and all the commuting back and forth."

"I'm the one who should thank you for showing this property to your sisters," Max says.

I hold up my palms. "Okay, okay. This wasn't all men's decisions. I had planned on staying here to oversee the inn part-time."

Wyatt jerks his head, and Max follows, the two of them speaking in low tones.

I widen my eyes. Is Wyatt giving Max some kind of fatherly advice about me? I lift my gown and hurry to catch up with them just as I hear Wyatt say, "I knew you were cool when Scout went crazy for you."

Just then Scout breaks free from Skylar's grip and races toward us. His paws look a little dirty like he found a digging spot. Pond? Garden? I panic for a moment that he's going to ruin my wedding gown, but he only has eyes for Max. He races to him and promptly sits, waiting for a pet. Max gives him a vigorous pet that has Scout's tongue lolling happily.

I join them, and the photographer gets pictures of the three of us. My little family—me, Max, and Scout.

After the pictures are done, I turn to Max. "Maybe we should let eloping couples bring their dog to the event."

"Remember how Paige worried about pet allergies?" He wraps an arm around my shoulders. "This is just for us. They could bring kids though." His eyes are on his brother, Liam, bringing some food to his pregnant girlfriend, Alexis.

"Are you hoping Liam will marry her and their twins will be at the ceremony?"

"It would be cool." He snaps the lapels of his tux jacket. "I probably inspired him."

I smile. "Because you're a happily married man."

"Damn right. You think you might want a couple of kids of our own down the line?"

I hug him and beam. "I'd love that. But we're not naming them after you. Two Max Bellamys in the family is confusing enough."

"How about Maxine?"

I laugh. "We're going to circle back to that after I'm fully armed with a baby name book."

He gives me a tender smile, his blue eyes soft. "I look forward to everything with you."

We head back to our family and friends, hand in hand, the strength of our love binding us together on Lovers' Lane, where it all began.

Don't miss the next book in the series, *Chasing*, where Paige and Spencer strike a deal for a revenge wedding date that takes a wrong turn!

Paige

The problem with Spencer Wolf is that he thinks he's the boss when *I'm* the boss. I run the inn. He's my consultant chef and caterer, as well as an arrogant confirmed bachelor.

But when I break down over an invitation to my ex-fiancé's wedding, it's Spencer who steps in to the rescue, offering to be my revenge wedding date. The perfect doting fake husband.

The catch? He wants the honeymoon too. One night, no strings. No effing way!

And then he kisses me and, in a moment of lusty weakness, I agree.

Biggest mistake of my life. Pretty sure.

Spencer

Face it, Paige, you need me.

Sign up for my newsletter and never miss a new release!
kyliegilmore.com/newsletter

ALSO BY KYLIE GILMORE

Unleashed Romance <<steamy romcoms with dogs!

Fetching (Book 1)

Dashing (Book 2)

Sporting (Book 3)

Toying (Book 4)

Blazing (Book 5)

Chasing (Book 6)

Daring (Book 7)

Leading (Book 8)

Racing (Book 9)

Loving (Book 10)

The Clover Park Series <<brothers who put family first!

The Opposite of Wild (Book 1)

Daisy Does It All (Book 2)

Bad Taste in Men (Book 3)

Kissing Santa (Book 4)

Restless Harmony (Book 5)

Not My Romeo (Book 6)

Rev Me Up (Book 7)

An Ambitious Engagement (Book 8)

Clutch Player (Book 9)

A Tempting Friendship (Book 10)

Clover Park Bride: Nico and Lily's Wedding

A Valentine's Day Gift (Book 11)

Maggie Meets Her Match (Book 12)

The Clover Park STUDS series <<hawt geeks who unleash into studs!

Almost Over It (Book 1)

Almost Married (Book 2)

Almost Fate (Book 3)

Almost in Love (Book 4)

Almost Romance (Book 5)

Almost Hitched (Book 6)

Happy Endings Book Club Series <<the Campbell family and a romance book club collide!

Hidden Hollywood (Book 1)

Inviting Trouble (Book 2)

So Revealing (Book 3)

Formal Arrangement (Book 4)

Bad Boy Done Wrong (Book 5)

Mess With Me (Book 6)

Resisting Fate (Book 7)

Chance of Romance (Book 8)

Wicked Flirt (Book 9)

An Inconvenient Plan (Book 10)

A Happy Endings Wedding (Book 11)

The Rourkes Series <<swoonworthy princes and kickass princesses!

Royal Catch (Book 1)

Royal Hottie (Book 2)

Royal Darling (Book 3)

Royal Charmer (Book 4)

Royal Player (Book 5)

Royal Shark (Book 6)

Rogue Prince (Book 7)

Rogue Gentleman (Book 8)

Rogue Rascal (Book 9)

Rogue Angel (Book 10)

Rogue Devil (Book 11)

Rogue Beast (Book 12)

Check out my website for the most up-to-date list of my books:
kyliegilmore.com/books

ABOUT THE AUTHOR

Kylie Gilmore is the *USA Today* bestselling author of the Unleashed Romance series, the Rourkes series, the Happy Endings Book Club series, the Clover Park series, and the Clover Park STUDS series. She writes humorous romance that makes you laugh, cry, and reach for a cold glass of water.

Kylie lives in New York with her family, two cats, and a nutso dog. When she's not writing, reading hot romance, or dutifully taking notes at writing conferences, you can find her flexing her muscles all the way to the high cabinet for her secret chocolate stash.

Sign up for Kylie's Newsletter and get a FREE book! kyliegilmore.com/newsletter

For text alerts on Kylie's new releases, text KYLIE to the number (888) 707-3025. (US only)

For more fun stuff check out Kylie's website https://www.kyliegilmore.com.

Thanks for reading *Blazing.* I hope you enjoyed it. Would you like to know about new releases? You can sign up for my new release email list at kyliegilmore.com/newsletter. I promise not to clog your inbox! Only new release info, sales, and some fun giveaways.

I love to hear from readers! You can find me at:
kyliegilmore.com
Instagram.com/kyliegilmore
Facebook.com/KylieGilmoreToo
Twitter @KylieGilmoreToo

If you liked Max and Brooke's story, please leave a review on your favorite retailer's website or Goodreads. Thank you.

Made in the USA
Las Vegas, NV
15 April 2022

47553895R00095